I0700734

Cozy Up
to Danger

a novel about heists,
hostages, a cat, and snacks

by Colin Conway

Cozy Up to Danger

Copyright © 2022 Colin Conway

ISBN: 979-8-9859409-8-5

Cover design by Zach McCain

Original Ink Press,
  an imprint of High Speed Creative, LLC
1521 N. Argonne Road, #C-205
Spokane Valley, WA 99212

Visit the author's website at www.colinconway.com

For Nana

"This job would be great if it
wasn't for the #$@!% customers."

Randal Graves (Jeff Anderson)/
Clerks

Cozy Up to Danger

a novel about heists,
hostages, a cat, and snacks

Chapter 1

When the store's electronic bell warbled, Ned Delahanty looked up from behind the counter where he stood counting cigarettes. The customer who entered the Quik N Go brought along a blast of cold air. The man didn't bother to shut the door behind him, and a gust of snow blew in.

The customer was in his early thirties and had the self-important look of someone who grew up wealthy. His eyes carried too much confidence for a face filled with flaccid features. He wasn't fat, but his pale skin hung loosely from his cheeks and his bulbous nose drooped as if from its own weight.

Next to Ned, an orange cat shifted its resting place on a nearby chair. He must have sensed the sudden entrance of cold air because his ears pulled back, and he tucked his head under Ned's red winter coat, which rested over the back of the chair.

"Evening," Ned said without breaking his count. *Thirty-two, thirty-three, thirty-four...*

The customer smirked as his gaze swept over the convenience store. He wore a blue winter coat, lighter blue snow pants, and a red knitted hat with a ridiculous fuzzy ball on top. Thick blue gloves covered his hands.

Advertisements for cigarettes, beer, and

sodas littered the building's large glass windows. All that visual clutter didn't stop Ned from seeing the green Land Rover Defender parked near the front of the building. Its headlights blazed against the advertising clutter. Two pairs of snow skis were attached to its roof rack. A woman sat in the passenger seat with her head bowed as if she might be reading something. She wore a tan knit hat with a fuzzy ball on top.

The customer aggressively stamped the snow from his boots onto the front mat. The company's bright orange and blue logo was mostly worn off from years of shuffling and stomping feet, and now the only thing left was a muddy *Q Go*.

The gas station's illuminated pylon sign was barely discernible at the edge of the parking lot, and heavy snowfall obscured the company's logo. The lower sign announced *Available bungalows for rent! Cheap!* but was wholly unreadable from the store.

There were five units in the back, and Ned lived in one. The other four hadn't rented since he started working there. That no longer surprised him since the units weren't visible from the highway. With a ski resort forty-five minutes north and another an hour beyond that, folks simply drove by to the nicer accommodations.

When the customer finished clearing the snow from his boots, he studied Ned. He slipped off his gloves and jerked his head toward the front windows. "You should clear the sidewalk. It's treacherous."

Ned finished his tally, jotted the number onto a nearby notepad, and leaned onto the counter.

"The snow is coming down something fierce." The customer motioned toward the window again. "Look at that."

Great White's "Once Bitten" played through a pair of tinny speakers mounted at opposite ends of the shop. Ned knew the song intimately from its repeated playing on this radio station.

The customer indignantly brushed the snow away from his shoulders. The powder fell beyond the mat to the store's linoleum floor. "Hey, bud, did you hear me? Are you deaf or something?" The man scrunched his face and looked toward the speakers. "And what's with this old fogey music?"

"Something you looking for?" Ned put the cigarettes under the counter.

The customer rolled his eyes as he approached. The soles of his boots squeaked with each step. "Did you hear what I said about the sidewalk?"

Ned stood on his tiptoes and looked outside. The snow *was* accumulating fast. It appeared there might be close to more than six inches on the sidewalk now. He dropped to his regular height. "It can wait."

The man's eyes widened. "That's a blizzard out there, and you've got paying customers showing up." He tapped his chest. "You saw me slip—right?"

Ned shook his head. "You didn't slip."

"I almost did."

"But you didn't."

"I could have."

Ned raised his eyebrows.

The customer pointed outside. "Didn't anyone teach you about limiting potential risk hazards?"

"No." Ned motioned toward the shovel near the front door. "But help yourself."

The customer eyed the yellow plastic tool, then pulled back in mock horror. "Me?"

"If it bothers you so much."

"But it's not my job."

"So?"

"So?" The man's voice rose dramatically. "*So?*" Now, he tapped his chest with both hands. "I'm the customer."

"What's that got to do with it?"

"I'm always right."

Ned smirked. "Not here."

"Most definitely here." The man looked around the store. "You should treat me like gold. It doesn't look like you're brimming with customers."

Ned shrugged. "We're doing all right."

The man's shoulders slumped. "Listen, bud. Even in the middle of nowhere, the customer is always right. That's what they teach guys with an MBA." He set his hand over his heart and tried to affect a look of humility. It melted into a glare of derision. "Maybe you missed that in business school."

Ned put his notepad and pencil away.

"You know what else they taught us in business school?" The customer turned toward the shovel, and his shoes gleefully squeaked. "MBAs don't shovel anything."

"They shovel something," Ned muttered.

"What'd you say?"

"Nothing."

The customer pointed at the shovel. "That, my friend, is a tool for guys without a high school diploma."

Ned straightened to his full height, which was several inches taller than the customer. He crossed his thick arms over his chest. The man's attention was drawn to the inky ball of fire on the back of Ned's right hand. It seemed to disappear underneath the long-sleeve t-shirt that Ned wore.

The customer's gaze traveled up to Ned's scowl. He nervously chuckled. "Heh-heh, but college isn't for everyone. Am I right?"

Ned cocked his head.

"Everyone's got a different route to success." The customer flashed a grin filled with perfectly white teeth. "You know what? We've gotten off on the wrong foot. Forget the snow." The customer waved at the window. "My name's Donovan." He took another couple of squeaky steps forward and extended his hand. When Ned didn't shake it, the man giggled uncertainly. "Totally understand. People come to Eagle's Feet to ski, right? If they can't handle the snow, that's their problem." Donovan eyed the storm outside, then stood on his tiptoes. His boots squeaked again. "I say leave the sidewalk as it is. It adds to the ambiance." Donovan dropped to his regular height and put his hands on his hips. He nodded approvingly. "Now that I think about it, the snow on the sidewalk is perfect."

Ned repeated his earlier question. "Something you looking for?"

Donovan's smile faltered, and he turned to Ned. He scratched his neck when he asked, "The restroom?"

"Paying customers only."

"But we don't need gas." The guy pointed to the Land Rover. "It's a hybrid with insane gas mileage." He spread his arms wide and drew out the word 'insane' in the way a used car salesman might. Donovan smiled, and a look of piousness flashed over his face. "It's the least we could do for the environment."

"I'm sure."

Donovan started to say something but stopped. His mouth slowly hung open, and his brow furrowed.

"Store policy." Ned pointed to a nearby sign. It read *Restroom for Paying Customers ONLY. No exceptions.* "You don't need to buy gas. Anything will do."

Donovan nodded knowingly. "You're extorting the customers."

Ned shrugged.

"But in a nice way." Donovan cleared his throat. "I get it. Are you sure you didn't go to business school? You're a natural." He bent to inspect the various food items along the front counter shelf. "What do we have here?" he said to himself.

Displayed were miscellaneous candy bars, donuts, gum, and nuts.

Overhead, the music ended, and a cheerful announcer interrupted. "*All right, all right, how about that sweet classic, dudes and dudettes? That's when metal was bodacious and smelled of hairspray. What a totally fantastic time! This is Headbanger Harv, and I'll be rocking you into the morning on Classic 106.9 FM.*"

Donovan smirked disapprovingly. "Metal," he muttered.

"*Now the news.*" The announcer cleared his throat and adopted a serious tone. "*Officials in Casper continue to interview witnesses in the daring robbery of the National Bank of Wyoming. Details are vague. No reports on how much money was stolen and no suspect descriptions have been provided as of yet.*" Headbanger Harv's tone switched back to playful. "*Lame. The cops are really on top of that one. Hello, McFly? Let's see if they can get us any more details before tomorrow. Let's forget all that with this radical rip from Trixter!*"

A guitar riff pierced the store's quiet, and Donovan grimaced. Ned was about to agree with his assessment of the band, but the man motioned toward the shelf full of goodies.

"What's with this garbage? It's all sugar and wheat except the nuts but imagine the calories that those have." He flicked his hand at the shelf's contents. "We can't eat any of this. What do we look like—animals?" Donovan lifted his chin in the direction of the sleeping tom. "Would you let your cat eat this junk?"

"He eats mice."

Donovan's face soured. "You get what I'm saying."

"Don't buy anything," Ned said. "The mountain is forty-five minutes away."

"Not in this weather." Donovan turned toward the window. "With this snow, it's gonna take forever. I'm afraid they might even close it."

"They can close a mountain?"

Donovan eyed him suspiciously. "The whole highway, too. How do you not know this?"

Ned shrugged. "Head back to Casper then. It's flat the entire way. Should be easy."

The customer danced an impatient jig. "The roads are still gonna be slow, and that manhunt is underway. The cops will be everywhere." As an afterthought, he added, "No, thank you."

Ned stared at him.

Donovan's shoulders wriggled back and forth. "C'mon, bud. Cut me some slack—just this once."

"If I do it for you..."

The customer leaned in, but Ned hadn't intended to finish his thought.

"Yeah?" Donovan asked. "If you do it for me?"

"I'd have to do it for everybody."

"What's wrong with that?" His finger flicked the sign. "That rule is stupid and only intended to stop the poor from using the restroom."

"You're not poor."

Donovan appeared offended, and he stopped his little dance. "How do you know? You don't." His face scrunched with righteous indignation. "You're judging me, and that's not right. You're customer profiling without verifiable data. You should know better. You work for a Fortune 500 company, and your actions reflect directly upon your employer."

Ned wanted to point out that anyone driving a new Land Rover to a Wyoming ski resort while bragging about an MBA wasn't likely to be poor. Instead, he said, "Using our restroom doesn't pay the bills."

"Sweet lord, bud. It's a restroom." Donovan threw his hands into the air. "It's not like it's a private viewing room at the Louvre."

Ned had no idea where the Louvre was, but he'd heard of private viewing rooms at other strip clubs. He pointed at the nearby sign and repeated the store's policy. "Paying customers only."

"That so?" Donovan's head bobbed from left to right. "What's stopping me from walking back there right now and using it? What are you gonna do about it?"

"Nothing."

The customer laughed confidently and backpedaled a few squeaky steps. "So you realize how stupid and unenforceable your rule is?"

"It's locked," Ned said. "You need a key."

Donovan's expression flattened, and he returned to the counter like a chastised child. "Why didn't you say so from the beginning?" He reconsidered the shelf of goodies. He grabbed a bag of peanuts and slapped them onto the counter. "I'll take these."

Ned entered the item into the cash register and announced a total.

"Only in America," Donovan said, "can a man be held hostage by the proletariat just to use the restroom." He pulled out his wallet, then slipped a black credit card from its resting spot. He proudly held up the small piece of plastic and waved it back and forth. "Ever see one of these?"

Ned pointed to another handwritten sign— *Cash only for purchases under five dollars.*

Donovan snatched his credit card back and hollered, "You gotta be kidding!" His face reddened. "You're only doing this to—"

"Watch it," Ned said. He pointed to yet one more sign—*No Swearing.*

"Are you for real? I gotta pay to use the restroom, *and* I can't swear in here? Who died and made you king?"

"Store policy."

Donovan frowned. He angrily marched to the front door. He put his hand on the horizontal handle but looked back to Ned. "I'm dying here, bud. *Please.*"

Ned stared at him.

"A person can develop long-term, serious side-effects from not using a bathroom on time."

"I've heard."

"You don't care." Donovan let go of the door, and his eyes narrowed. "It's because I complained about the sidewalks, isn't it?"

"I don't know what you're talking about."

"I said—"

"I know what you said." He motioned toward the signs again. "Store policy."

Donovan grunted once, then hurried toward the coolers. A moment later, he returned to the counter with four bottles of water. At the counter, he plonked them down. "This is the least offensive thing in this store."

"Present company included," Ned said.

"Right." Donovan's head popped up. "Wait. What?"

Ned rang the first bottle of water up.

The customer grabbed one of the bottles. As he did so, he shuffled from one foot to the other. "We gotta be extra careful, so this plastic doesn't end up in the ocean."

Ned tapped the enter button on the register to repeat the transaction.

"Because that happens, you know?" Donovan's gyrations continued as he waggled a plastic bottle for Ned to see. "There's this massive ball of plastic out in the Pacific and—"

Ned's finger hovered over the cash register as he stared at the customer.

"Why did you stop?" Donovan's dance intensified. Beads of sweat formed on his forehead. He set down the water bottle and put both hands on the counter's edge. "My kidneys are under duress."

Ned tapped the enter button twice more. When he finished totaling the waters up, he pointed at the bag of nuts. "Still want the peanuts?"

"No, I don't want them." Donovan angrily slid the bag to the side. "I never wanted them. What is your problem?"

"If you don't get them, the total doesn't come to five, and you can't—"

"I'll take the peanuts!" Donovan slid the small bag back toward the bottles. "What's the total now?"

Ned announced the amount, and Donovan jammed his credit card into the processing machine.

"What's taking so long?" He shuffled from side to side. "This thing on dial-up or something?"

"Probably the weather."

The machine beeped its acceptance of the credit card, and relief flooded Donovan's face. He held out his hand. "The key. Let's go."

Ned ripped off the receipt and handed it to Donovan. "The restroom's out of order."

The customer's face whitened. "What?"

"It broke yesterday."

Donovan ran to the rear of the store. His boots chirped across the linoleum floor as he went. When he reached the restroom door, he stopped and stared at it. "You gotta be kidding me!"

Ned knew what Donovan was looking at since he'd placed the out-of-order sign there last night. A piece inside the toilet had broken, and he hadn't had a chance to go to Casper for a replacement part.

"What's wrong with you?" the customer hollered. As he hurried back toward Ned, Donovan said, "You couldn't have told me this when I walked in?"

"I could have, but you wanted to complain about the snow."

Donovan stopped and clenched his fists. "I knew this was about the sidewalks!" He glanced frantically around. "What am I supposed to do now?"

"You can rent one of the bungalows."

The customer's face widened with surprise. "An upsell? *Now?*" He grunted an expletive as he headed for the door.

Ned tapped the *No Swearing* sign, figuring that verbally correcting the man at the moment might be bad form.

Donovan yanked open the door. Another blast of cold air entered the store. "Shovel the stupid sidewalks!" A gust of snow blew across the entry mat.

"Don't forget your waters," Ned said pleasantly.

"I never wanted them in the first place!"

"Want me to refund the purchase? It should only take a couple minutes, but I don't really know for sure. I've never done one before."

Donovan muttered a second expletive as more snow floated into the store. The man stepped outside and angrily clomped his way toward his Land Rover. Just as he turned to yell at Ned through the window, his feet slipped out from underneath him, and he fell.

Ned stood on his tiptoes to look out the window. Donovan lay prostrate in the snow. The guy had been right. The sidewalk was treacherous. Perhaps Ned should go out and shovel it.

Donovan hurriedly stood and brushed the snow from his clothes. Then he angrily shook his fist at Ned. Standing in the storm while illuminated by his vehicle's headlights, Donovan looked like a performer in some strange music video. It didn't hurt that a bad eighties rock song continued to play through the store's speakers like a soundtrack.

The woman in the Land Rover yelled something to Donovan, and he stopped shaking his fist. After he climbed into the vehicle, it backed away from the building. The SUV pulled out of the lot, entered the highway, and headed north.

Ned watched it disappear into the blizzard. He thought about driving into the snowstorm. "Better him than me."

Chapter 2

Ned leaned his elbows on the counter and watched a family at the nearest gas pump. The canopy's high-powered lights reflected off the hood of their silver Lincoln Navigator. It seemed as if the family were in the middle of a fluorescent island surrounded by deep darkness. Occasionally, a gust of wind blew a sheet of white powder sideways and under the metal overhang.

A woman in her mid-thirties stood in the middle of four young girls—a mother duck and her ducklings. The kids ranged from three to six years. Ned had gotten good at guessing the ages of children due to his previous job as a mall Santa Claus.

The girls laughed as they danced and skipped underneath their mother's outstretched arms. The children wore light purple snow gear, pink knitted hats, and pink boots. Their mother wore clothes in the opposite—pink snow gear with a light purple stocking cap and light purple boots. It seemed all their winter clothing had been dragged through a cotton candy machine.

Next to the gas pump stood the father. He was dressed in stark contrast to his family, wearing a black ski suit, black cap, and black snow boots. He frowned and ruefully shook his head at what Ned assumed was the unsuppressed chatter of four excited girls.

When the fueling ended, the father shoved the gas nozzle back into the pump. Sensing some conclusion to the process, the children jumped and clapped in unison. Their mother immediately shooed them toward the store. The girls sprinted awkwardly across the parking lot and through the rapidly accumulating snow. Their oversized boots forced them to lift their feet higher than necessary and take the occasional, elongated jump. They laughed and held their arms out for balance.

At the building, the girls had trouble opening the front door. They impatiently waved and called for their mother to hurry along. She, however, waited under the canopy for her husband. After he snatched a receipt from the gas pump, he dutifully kissed his wife on the cheek, and the couple headed toward the store. The husband and wife leaned into the wind as they passed through the blowing snowstorm.

The children hopped and squealed with excitement as their parents approached.

Ned straightened and muttered one of the few expletives he ever allowed himself to say. "Kids."

The mother jerked the door open, and the children burst inside. Never had the doorbell's pathetic warble held more meaning. The girls' yelping and chattering drowned out the store's music. Helix's "Rock You" played through the poor-quality speakers. The kids fanned out through the store like an underaged hit squad.

"Stay together," the mother implored, but it

went unheeded as the children scattered further apart.

The youngest ran immediately for the hats displayed on a wire spinner. There were orange beanies and blue trucker hats. Both featured the Quik N Go logo. The child stared at the various head garments with awe.

The second youngest skipped over to the magazine rack. She dropped to her knees, grabbed an issue of *Warbirds*, and gleefully flipped through it.

Ned watched the third child as she stalked toward the front counter like a lioness sneaking up on a gazelle. The girl's eyes twinkled with delight as she marveled at a rack filled with plastic keychains, lucky rabbits' feet, and printed magnets.

From the candy aisle, the oldest child exclaimed, "Over here!" She lifted her arm like an explorer announcing a historic find. The other girls shrieked, quickly abandoned their own discoveries, and tromped in her direction.

The parents took time stamping the snow from their boots. They carefully wiped the accumulation of powder from each other's shoulders. Rapidly melting snow covered the store's entry mat. The mother pecked her husband on the lips and went in search of her children. The father turned, made eye contact with Ned, and headed toward the counter.

"How you doing?" he asked.

"What can I get you?"

When the children screamed with glee, the

father winced. "Earplugs?"

"All out."

"Of course." The father glanced over his shoulder. When his attention returned to Ned, he surreptitiously placed a fifty-dollar bill on the counter. He whispered, "A pack of reds, but be quiet about it."

Ned reached above his head, pulled a box of Marlboro's from the cigarette rack, and set them on the counter. The father slipped the small package into his pocket.

"Ring them up when the girls come over with their candy."

Ned nodded.

"Alden," the woman called. "Would you like something? They've got Peppermint Patties."

"I'm good," the father said. "Thank you, Hattie."

The woman rose as if standing on her tiptoes and eyed her husband. "What are you doing over there?"

"Nothing, dear," he said. "Just asking directions."

She rolled her eyes and then returned to her regular height.

The oldest girl ran by her mother and was followed by the younger siblings. The clomping of their boots carried its own frenetic rhythm.

"Girls," Hattie muttered half-heartedly. Her attention seemed to be on the shelf of candy. "No running."

Overhead, the music stopped, and the announcer came on. "*Whoa, dudes and dudettes! How about that one? Headbanger Harv here, and I'm gonna rock you through this gnarly blizzard—only on Classic 106.9 FM."* The announcer cleared his throat, and his voice dropped an octave in officiousness. *"Back to our breaking news story."*

Alden looked toward the speakers.

"Authorities believe that the robbers of the Casper National Bank of Wyoming are still in the immediate vicinity."

Hattie straightened. "Girls, come here right now."

The children had once again fanned out through the store. Now, two girls stood in front of the hat rack. Two others were at the magazines. All moaned their displeasure.

"Don't you 'oh' me," Hattie said. "We're not getting candy for my health."

Alden eyed his wife. She noticed his look and shrugged.

"Due to the historic storm," Harv continued, *"tracking the suspects has been sporadic and difficult. According to authorities, the suspects are driving a late-model Chevy van. No description of the suspects has yet been provided."*

Alden made no move to help his wife corral the children. Instead, he watched his girls with a mild fascination—the way safari attendees might watch hungry hyenas circle a wounded zebra.

Headbanger Harv's public safety announcement continued. *"If you encounter these individuals, an abundance of caution is advised. They are considered armed and extremely dangerous.*" Harv's voice returned to its normal level of playfulness. "*It's totally bogus how the cops are handling this. Like, they should take a chill pill. It's not like these airheads will get far in this storm. Did they not check the weather report? Duh. Anyway, let's get back to the good times with Jackyl's monster hit, 'The Lumberjack.'*"

A chainsaw briefly roared through the low-grade speakers. The four girls all stopped what they were doing and turned their faces toward the ceiling. When a guitar riff began, they howled with amusement. The children skipped through the aisles with their lips buzzing.

"Headed up to the mountain?" Ned said. It seemed a polite thing to ask now that the store's music had turned the children into chainsaw-buzzing maniacs.

Alden lifted an eyebrow. "What gave you that idea?"

Ned shrugged. "Making conversation."

"Sorry." Alden waved a dismissive hand. "It's been a long drive."

The girls collectively buzzed and pretended to cut down anything near them. One of them mimed chopping down a cardboard caricature of the Cheetos cat.

"Girls!" Hattie said, "stop that this instant and pick out your candy."

"Where you from?" Ned asked. He'd learned recently that these were the things people did to be polite. They asked silly questions with answers no one cared about.

"South Dakota," Alden said. He looked over his shoulder to check on his family. "We're heading up to the mountain for the week."

The four children spun through the aisles amid their roaring chainsaw sounds. Now, three of them stood at the hat spinner. They each studied the hats like they were preparing for a test. The fourth girl stood in the automotive aisle. Her lips reverberated as she studied a bottle of motor oil.

Alden wriggled his fingers. "Better make it one more."

Ned reached up for a second pack of cigarettes.

The father secreted this box into a different pocket. He turned fully to Ned now and lowered his voice. "I gotta sneak outside to smoke these. Can you believe that? A grown man." He leaned an elbow on the counter, and his gaze drifted down to his hand. "The girls were easier when they were younger. Of course, there was less of them then." Alden snickered, but the self-conscious chuckle quickly cut off. His attention snapped to Ned. "Not that I would trade any of them." He cleared his throat and turned back to his family. "Can't say that. Never. No."

One of the girls shrieked amid the others' buzzing chainsaw sounds.

"Enough," Hattie said. "Stop that noise right now, or we're leaving, and you're not getting any candy."

It was as if the chainsaws suddenly ran out of gas. The girls, however, did not. The children returned to skipping through the aisles. Somehow, they each selected something on a pass through the candy section. All waved their choice in the air as if they were part of some synchronized dance squad.

"Please, girls," Hattie implored, "hurry up and pick your second. It's time to go."

Alden spun toward his children and sternly said, "Ladies!"

The children froze in whatever position they happened to be in and stared with wide eyes at their father. One girl held a candy bar over her head like a killer wielding a knife in a slasher film while another reared back in mock alarm. The third child balanced on one leg while the other extended behind her in an awkward yoga pose. The final kid—the youngest—squatted as if about to jump. None of the girls dared move, and they all remained focused upon their patriarch.

"We need to beat the storm," Alden calmly said. "They might close the mountain. You know what that means?"

The children nodded solemnly.

"You don't want to get stuck in the car, do you?"

The four girls shook their heads.

"Then pick up the pace." He smacked his hands together. "Get your other candy. Go."

Smiles spread across their faces a millisecond before the children squealed. The fourth child finished her leap, and the chase began again.

"Girls!" Hattie shouted. "Girls!" She looked pleadingly at her husband.

He shrugged. "I tried." Alden turned his head slightly and spoke over his shoulder. "Make it another."

Ned reached up and retrieved a third pack of Marlboro's.

"Pretty nasty storm." Alden slipped the latest packet of cigarettes into a pocket. "Might break some records." He eyed Ned. "Best thing that could happen is we get snowed in for the week."

"But you'll be stuck in a room with them."

Alden's brow furrowed. "What're you implying?"

"Nothing."

The wrinkle in the father's forehead deepened. "I like my kids." It sounded as if he were trying to convince himself.

"I was just saying."

"I know what you're saying." Alden nodded. "And this isn't my first rodeo. I can spot an upsell when it's being made."

It was the second time today that Ned had been accused of such a thing. He'd never been to business school and didn't want any of that stuffed-shirt stuff rubbing off on him. "That's not what I'm doing," he said. "Trust me."

"Sure, sure, and now you're trying to get me to trust you. Get the customer to buy into what you're selling. Kudos to you, guy. It worked." He waved his hand. "One more."

Ned pulled another pack of cigarettes from

the rack and placed it on the counter.

The box disappeared into Alden's pocket. "Keeping count?" he asked.

"Four."

"Should be enough." Alden nodded with approval. "So, you ski?"

"Never."

Alden glanced over his shoulder to watch his family. "You're lucky."

"You don't like it?"

"Hate it."

"Then why are you going up for a week?"

Alden eyed Ned knowingly. "That's a question only an unmarried man asks."

Ned turned his palms up in a what-could-he-say gesture.

The father's eyes took on a wistful look, and a dreamy smile spread across his lips. "I was once like you." He blinked and shook his head. "Nope. Can't think like that."

The girls hopped about the candy aisle and chanted, "Chocolate, ba-colate, gonna get some chocolate."

"I'm serious," Hattie said. "This is my last warning."

Alden said, "All right, ladies, wrap it up. We're running out of time."

The children tossed their candy bars to each other now. Ned had seen similar acts while in Las Vegas.

Without looking at Ned, Alden motioned toward him and wriggled his fingers.

Ned reached above his head and pulled down

a fifth pack of cigarettes. Like the others before, this one vanished into a pocket.

"What's with the bungalows?" Alden asked. "We saw them listed on the sign."

"They're out back."

Alden cast a sideways glance. "Get many takers? It seems an odd place for a motel if you know what I mean? Out here in the middle of nowhere. It's like the beginning of a horror movie or something."

"It's not so bad," Ned said. "It's usually quiet."

No one had rented one of the bungalows since he'd started working at the store. He'd already cleaned the units because he was bored. And he thought it might be interesting to have someone stay there, just to break the monotony of the days. If this repetitiveness was what he felt after a few weeks, how would it be after several months?

Or worse, a year?

As if a dog whistle had been blown, the children hurried toward their father. Each now had two pieces of candy. They excitedly slapped them onto the counter.

"Can we get a hat?" the oldest asked.

The other three girls bounced with excitement and yelled variations of "Yeah!"

"Not this time," Alden said.

"If we come back?" the oldest asked.

"Sure." Alden winked at Ned. "If we come back, you each can get a hat."

The girls shouted with glee. The youngest girl noticed the tom sleeping on the chair next to

Ned and squealed, "A cat!" This led to all the girls bouncing like snapping pieces of popcorn. The tom lifted its head, jumped off the chair, and hurried away to someplace quieter.

Ned eyed the approaching Hattie. "Anything for you?"

"If you can't beat 'em." She slipped a candy bar onto the counter. "You sure you don't want anything?" she asked her husband.

Alden shook his head. "Nothing for me, no."

Ned finished ringing up the candy and announced a total nearing forty-five dollars.

Hattie's eyes widened. "For nine pieces of candy?"

"Inflation," Alden said and held out his hand toward Ned. "It's getting ridiculous."

"I guess."

Hattie passed out the candy to her children and then pushed them toward the door. The girls burst into more shouts of joy. When the band of little marauders stomped their way outside, the doorbell announced their departure with an electronic warble of hope.

A gentler calm returned as Autograph's "Turn Up the Radio" played through the speakers.

Ned counted out Alden's change.

The father swooped up the money and slipped it into his pocket. "Wish me luck." He left the store and crossed the snow-covered parking lot. He helped the four girls into the vehicle before climbing in himself.

Ned watched the whole production and could think only one thing—*better him than me.*

Chapter 3

"Better you than me," U.S. Marshal Gayle Goodspeed said.

Beauregard Smith looked up from his Caveman burger. He had ordered the entree out of habit, though he wasn't particularly hungry. Beau was checking out the burger's slathering of barbecue sauce and its three strips of bacon when Goodspeed spoke.

"What's that?" he asked.

She pointed her fork at his lunch. "That heart stopper." Her attention returned to her salad which she dutifully rotated with the utensil. "Better you than me."

They were at Grump's, a regional chain restaurant. This particular establishment was its Lincoln, Nebraska location, which was the first ever. A sign in the lobby had proudly proclaimed that fact.

Eclectic memorabilia hung from the walls—a child's tricycle, a wooden fishing boat, and a hunting rifle were some of the items displayed. A set of tracks ran around the top of the restaurant, and a toy train passed every few minutes. Its long trail of cars carried more memorabilia—a deflated football, an old boot, and a mannequin head. Everything seemed designed to provide a customer with sensory overload.

The restaurant was noisy as laughing families spoke loudly over an irritatingly cheerful pop song played through hidden speakers.

"Do you ski?" the marshal asked.

Beau wasn't sure he'd heard Goodspeed's question correctly. He leaned in. "Say again?"

The marshal stopped poking at her salad and swiveled the fork in her hand. Holding the utensil in the middle of her fist, she stabbed it several times into the table. "You know? Ski. That thing people do in the snow."

Beau shook his head. "Never been."

"Figures."

"Do you?"

Goodspeed flipped the fork back to its regular position. "Of course. Not anymore, but I've been. Plenty of times."

Beau estimated the marshal to be in her sixties—still young enough to ski. Physically, she seemed too old for the law enforcement job, but she was more cantankerous than most folks. She'd already proved that to him many times. Even though she appeared frail, Beau wasn't about to test her again. He was tired of losing.

"What did you mean by that?" Beau asked. "Figures. What figures?"

Goodspeed shoved a forkful of salad into her mouth. Speaking through her food, she said, "Look at you." Ranch dressing dribbled down her chin.

"What's wrong with me?"

"You're not the skiing type."

"Because I'm big?"

The marshal swallowed and then wiped her chin with a cloth napkin. "Big's got nothing to do with it. Plenty of big people ski. Weightlifters ski. So do the fat. Even tall people ski, although they look like they shouldn't."

"Then what? Are you saying I'm not coordinated enough to ski because I am, you know?"

She chuckled. "Sure, you are."

Beau's face warmed at the slight. So what if he hadn't played sports as a kid? And no one cared if he didn't play sports as an adult. He knew he was coordinated. At least, he *felt* coordinated. Beau could ride a motorcycle, and he could fight, and he could—

He stalled as he tried to think of other things he could do that required coordination. Shooting, he thought. Firing weapons required hand-eye coordination. He was a darn good shot. So, yeah, Beau Smith figured he was coordinated in all the things that mattered.

Goodspeed must have noticed the look on his face. "Relax, Little Sister."

Beau's face warmed further. He hated when she called him that. It was a thing she did to get under his skin, and it worked. He thought it would have stopped by now since they had established a pecking order with her firmly at the top, but Goodspeed continued to needle him.

She was his witness inspector, and her duty was to oversee his protection. Goodspeed wasn't his first inspector. That honor went to Theodore 'Ted' Onderdonk, who got shot helping Beau escape the Satan's Dawgs, the motorcycle club he turned rat on.

Onderdonk had a habit of needling Beau, too. Only Onderdonk did it through physical intimidation. Goodspeed did it through name-calling and mental trickery. Beau liked Onderdonk's way better; he liked his battles straight on.

Beau wanted to tell Goodspeed that he didn't appreciate it when she called him that name, but he knew doing so would make him sound like a whiner, a loser, a baby. He kept his mouth shut.

"You're not the skiing type—" Goodspeed waved her fork, which now had a baby tomato stuck on its tongs. "—because you're a Dawg."

"*Was* a Dawg."

"I stand corrected."

The Satan's Dawgs were the biker gang Beau belonged to before entering the witness protection program. The Dawgs had unique titles for those in positions of authority, and Beau was their bookkeeper. He was responsible for 'keeping book' on those who crossed the club. When the club decided it was time to 'clear the books," it was Beau's responsibility to do so. He had done many violent tasks in the name of the club. He no longer wanted to do such a thing because he believed the Dawgs had lost their way. Turning informant wasn't as hard as he'd expected when the FBI called.

Now, Beau wanted to be better than the man he used to be. Some of that desire started with him, but the rest of the change was inspired by a woman he had met during his first witness protection assignment. Even though he only spent a few days in Maine, he couldn't get Daphne Winterbourne out of his mind.

"But you can't ski," Goodspeed said.

"Lots of people can't ski."

"Know any bikers who *can?*"

Beau didn't need to think long about it. He leaned back in his booth and stared at her.

Goodspeed triumphantly harrumphed. "Thought so." She returned to pushing her salad about. "All my ideas are good ideas, Beau. When will you learn?"

He picked up a French fry, considered it, then put it back. "So, I'm going someplace cold. Great." He bolted forward. "It better not be Minnesota."

She grinned.

Beau leaned in further and pointed at her. "I'm telling you right now, Marshal, if you send me to Minnesota, I'm outta here. I won't stand for it."

"You're adorable when you get worked up."

"I'm serious," he said. "I'll quit the program and take my chances out there." He thumbed over his shoulder. "Minnesota is as bad as prison. Worse even."

"Little Sister," Goodspeed stabbed a hunk of lettuce, "sending you to Minnesota would be cruel and unusual punishment. We're not in the habit of doing that around here."

"You once named me Skeeter."

The marshal pointed the leaf-covered fork at Beau. "That was neither cruel nor unusual."

"Says you."

"That's right. I do. Skeeter was a fine name. You should have treated it with more respect."

Beau flicked a French fry with his finger.

"Not going to eat?" she asked.

"I'm waiting to hear where you're sending me. I might not have an appetite after."

"You could always learn to ski. They got classes, you know? If they can teach a kid, they can teach a lug like you." She pointed her hands toward each other. "Snowplow, Beau. You'd look good making that pizza slice down the hill." She cackled to herself.

He leaned an elbow on the table and rested his chin in his hand. "Why can't you send me someplace warm? Florida or Texas, maybe."

"Yeah, no."

"Why not?"

"You tell me one Dawg who skis, and I'll change your assignment." She smirked. "Go ahead. Gimme a name, and I'll send you to Miami. I hear it's beautiful down there."

Beau's brow furrowed.

"Night clubs, beaches, girls in bikinis. You like girls in bikinis, don't you, Beau? I'd bet a month's pay that those girls would like a handsome fella like you, too."

When he scowled, Goodspeed laughed.

"Don't hurt yourself, Little Sister. I did the

research, so I know I'm right."

Beau knew she was right, too. The Satan's Dawg's were from Phoenix, Arizona. They were a warm weather club and rode twelve months a year. They never went anywhere cold. It was one of the things he liked while he was part of the crew.

He hated to admit it, but he understood Goodspeed's reasoning for assigning him somewhere cold. He might change his mind after he knew where he was going, though. "It's not going to snow all year, is it?"

Beau admitted he wasn't the best student of geography, but he didn't think there was an arctic climate within America's borders.

"Geez, settle down, will ya? No, it won't snow year-round."

"Is it Alaska?"

She looked up from her salad. "We'd have to drive through Canada to get there."

"And?"

"First of all, I'm not going to expose you to any more law enforcement than I need to, and we'd have to cross a border to get there. Read a map occasionally. Second, it's Canada. I'd rather remarry my second husband."

Beau relaxed. "So, where?"

"Eagle's Feet, Wyoming."

He paused when he heard the location. The weather was nice for part of the year in Wyoming, so maybe it wouldn't be so bad. And not too long ago, he'd rented a storage unit in Evanston and hidden a motorcycle there. That was while he was on the run from the Dawgs after he fled his first assignment in Maine. He wondered how far Eagle's Feet was from Evanston.

The marshal watched him with curiosity. "What are you thinking?"

He was pondering how he could get to his motorcycle. He didn't want to lose the protection that the marshal service provided, but in the unlikely event that the Satan's Dawgs ever found him, he wanted an option of an additional escape route.

Beau couldn't tell Goodspeed about its existence, though. He didn't think she would confiscate it, but the marshals would know where he would run if things ever got bad. He liked having a secret all to himself.

He picked up a French fry and studied it. "They've got skiing in Wyoming?"

"If they've got skiing in Minnesota, they've definitely got it in Wyoming. Haven't you ever heard of Jackson Hole? That place is world famous."

He had heard of it; the Dawgs rode through there one summer.

"But that's not what you were really thinking, Beau."

He gnawed on his lip. The question of how far Evanston was lingered, but he couldn't come out and just ask it. "Where's Eagle's Feet?"

"A little north of Colorado. A bit south of Montana. Near the base of the Walla Kiki Mountain."

She wasn't giving him anything useful. If he mentioned Evanston, he'd tip his hand. Beau wasn't sure if the previous marshal, Onderdonk, knew about the bike's storage. Maybe he did, and Beau's coyness wasn't necessary. But if he didn't, then Goodspeed was in the dark. It was better to remain silent about the motorcycle.

Beau said, "I've never heard of the Walla Kiki."

Goodspeed waved a dismissive hand. "Why would you? You're not a skier. And don't ask about the origin of the name. It's got something or other to do with regional tribal history. If you want to know more, ask one of the locals."

It seemed she didn't care about names associated with tribal origins any more than he did.

"So what?" Beau said. "I'm going to work at a lodge handing out skis and whatnot?"

Goodspeed shook her head. "You're going to run one of our businesses."

When Beau first entered the witness protection program, he ran a mystery bookstore in Maine. The U.S. Marshals owned the business, and all he had to do was keep his head down. Unfortunately, the Satan's Dawgs discovered him there. A similar thing happened in his next assignment, which was also a government-owned business. Since then, Beau had worked a couple of real jobs courtesy of Marshal Goodspeed, but he liked the autonomy the first two assignments gave him.

Working in a government-run business felt like Goodspeed finally believed in him. "That's great." He bowed his head slightly. "Thank you."

She toasted him with the sliced cucumber stuck to the end of her fork. "Don't think too much about it. We had an opening, and I plugged you in."

"What happened to the guy I'm replacing?"

"He got bit by a jackalope."

Beau's face scrunched.

"Those horned rabbits are all over the plains. Nasty, evil critters." Her front teeth clacked together.

He stared at Goodspeed.

She stuffed the sliced cucumber into her mouth and smiled. When Beau didn't join in her frivolity, she frowned. "Don't get your panties in a ruffle, Little Sister. I'm just playin' around. The previous guy died of old age. We should all be so lucky."

"You're getting pretty lucky yourself."

Goodspeed looked up from her salad. "You should talk nicer to your elders, especially when I can change this assignment."

His expression flattened. "What am I going to do?"

"Something you're uniquely qualified for."

"You're not going to tell me?"

Goodspeed spun her fork in small circles. "Take a guess."

"You're not hiring me to be a bookkeeper, are you?"

The marshal's eyes narrowed. "We most

certainly are not."

"The government has those, right? But you call them something else."

"We do, and they are."

"I don't want to do that," Beau said. "Just so we're clear."

She waved her fork about. "That's good because you can never keep book for us."

"I'm not qualified for much else."

"Sure, you are." Goodspeed pushed her salad around. "Think about it."

He did have a lot of experience with firearms. "Is it a gun store?"

The marshal guffawed. "You're not even supposed to be in a room with a gun."

"You could make an allowance."

"Get real. I don't even want you thinking about guns. If you see a squirt gun, I want you to avert your eyes. Guess again."

Beau didn't know what else might fit the description of 'uniquely qualified' unless it was a knife store.

Her lips pursed. "And it's not knives either. No weapons. Nothing that can hurt anybody."

"In that case."

Goodspeed studied him. "You give up too easy."

"I'm not giving up. Gimme a minute."

Perhaps it was something a little less specific. He liked motorcycles and could fix them as well as any mechanic. Maybe she was going to set him up in a shop focused on bikes. How cool would that be?

So far, he'd operated a mystery bookstore, a vintage record shop, been a handyman, and a mall Santa. Was he finally going to get to do something that he truly enjoyed? Hope rose in his chest, and he did something he rarely did— he smiled. He opened his mouth to venture a guess.

Goodspeed said, "No."

"How do you know what I was going to say?"

"You looked happy."

"I'm not going to be happy where I'm going?"

"Get real."

Beauregard Smith sulked. "Then I give."

U.S. Marshal Gayle Goodspeed set down her fork and interlaced her fingers. "You've pumped gas before, haven't ya?"

"You're making me a nozzle nerd?"

"Think bigger." Goodspeed lifted her chin. "You're gonna run the joint."

"A gas station?"

"As my mother used to tell me, customer service is its own reward." Her smile was sardonic.

He thought about it for a moment. He'd been to hundreds of stations in his lifetime. Most of the time, people got their gas at the pump and went on about their way. How bad could it be, really? Nothing interesting ever went on at a gas station.

"Maybe it won't be so bad," Beau said and popped a French fry into his mouth.

Chapter 4

Ned Delahanty dragged a mop lazily back and forth across the vinyl floor. He tried wiping up the melting snow from Alden and Hattie's clomping children, but it only spread the wetness. The floor would remain slick until it air dried.

He dropped the mop into the bucket and used the handle to steer it out of the way. Ned set its head against the wall, but the handle slowly fell in a wide arc until it flopped against a stack of soda cases. He grunted his disinterest in further dealing with the mop.

Ned entered the small storeroom where he collected a yellow *Wet Floor* sign. When he returned to the main area, he propped open the yellow plastic sign and set it near the front door.

A thought amused him then—he was concerned someone might slip. His former self—not the guy who pretended to be Santa or the one who was a maintenance man in Chicago—but the jerk who kept the books for the Dawgs—that guy wouldn't have cared if someone lost their footing and fell. That guy might have found it funny and laughed.

Ned was embarrassed to admit that now. His grandmother wouldn't have approved of the man he'd been had she known his true colors. However, she would probably like the man he was becoming now.

He loved Ma since she practically raised him. Paula, his biological mother, was more interested in drugs than in rearing a child. Ned didn't even know his father. That guy took off before Ned was born. The only thing Paula ever told him about his father was that the man was a swindler with a messiah complex.

Ned wished he could call Ma and check on her. He'd like to tell her that he was okay. Heck, he'd like to chat about nothing for a while in the way they used to do. He missed those conversations. But chatting with her now could put her life in jeopardy.

It was the same reason he couldn't call Daphne Winterbourne. He wanted to let her know that he thought about her often. It was silly for him to pine that way. She'd probably long forgotten him by now. It had been months since they met. Daphne was an attractive woman. She wouldn't be wistful over some guy who stumbled into her life and almost got her killed.

Thankfully, she didn't know about the second time he almost got her killed—when the Satan's Dawgs discovered that he'd addressed a couple of postcards to her while in Belfry, Oregon. He dealt with that matter in a permanent way, but he hoped to avoid situations like that in the future.

The cat walked through the store. He stopped near the glistening section of floor and studied it. The tom carefully touched the wetness with a paw, then disdainfully shook it. The cat turned and ambled toward the counter.

"It's only water, Travis. Don't be a sissy."

The tom ignored his challenge and disappeared behind a shelving unit.

Overhead, an eighties metal song played. It was something Ned had never heard before and he was thankful for it. It was too poppy for his liking, and he imagined the male lead singer wore spandex, eyeliner, and far too much hair spray.

Ned preferred his heavy metal harder and edgier, but this was the best channel the radio provided. Central Wyoming wasn't known as the thrash capital of America. Outside of this classic rock station, the choices were limited to seventies country music or talk radio—neither was something Ned could tolerate.

Unfortunately, the DJs on this classic rock channel leaned toward the worst of the eighties. Ned liked Megadeth, Metallica, and Iron Maiden—all were good bands of that decade. The radio hadn't played a single one of their songs yet, and he'd been at the Quik N Go for nearly a month. Maybe the station got their music from a discount bin somewhere. He didn't think radio stations bought albums anymore, but the idea of marked-down music was the only way some of this station's musical choices made sense.

Ned considered the sopping wet entry mat with its muddy orange *Q Go*. When Marshal Goodspeed assigned him to this location, he tried to understand his role so he could play his part. It wasn't until he was alone for a couple of days that it hit him. There were Quik N Go stores across the nation. Were they all owned by the government? If so, was everyone who worked in them a member of the witness protection program?

That seemed a risky proposition because if the mob found a witness working in one Quik N Go, wouldn't they check them all after that? Ned decided that this must be a franchised location. It only made the most sense.

Yet when had the government made sense? All bright ideas grew dimmer whenever politicians were involved. And any inventive process would slowly grind to a halt the more public servants were invited to participate.

Ned gave up worrying about whether the entire Quik N Go franchise system was under the umbrella of the witness protection program and only considered the Eagle's Feet location. For the marshals, this site seemed ideal. The small gas station was isolated on a Central Wyoming highway.

There were no high-speed diesel pumps for long-haul truckers, so it rarely attracted business. The only customers the station enticed were the occasional tourists on their way to or from the nearby ski resort. Otherwise, travelers continued onto Casper in the east or Evanston to the west.

To an actual entrepreneur, this Quik N Go site would likely fail. For the witness protection program, it was a clear winner.

A pair of headlights pierced the night sky and the falling snow. A red Ford F-150 Raptor drove through the parking lot. The beefy rig moved parallel with the building before reversing into a parking stall. Its wheels bumped into a concrete curb stop, and the truck bounced slightly.

In the pickup's back window were two white stickers. The one behind the driver's seat read *Ride or Die*. On the other side was one that read *Live it, Love it, Ride it.*

A man climbed out from behind the steering wheel and strolled toward the front door. He waited patiently as a woman slipped from the passenger's seat. She held a cell phone in her hand and slowly turned toward the gas island. The woman stayed that way for a moment.

She wore a form-fitting, black ski suit with gray tire tracks printed across her legs. He wore a fitted ski suit with red flames rising from the bottom of the pant legs. They were an attractive couple and appeared ready to strut down a fashion-show catwalk.

The man noticed Ned through the window and lifted his chin in a friendly greeting. Ned nodded back.

Eventually, the woman turned toward the building. She lifted the camera slightly above her head and talked while she walked.

Ned moved deeper into the store. He had a bad feeling about what was occurring.

The man opened the door, and the bell warbled weakly. As the woman entered, a blast of cold air and a flurry of snow blew in. The couple paused on the mat. The man brushed the snow from the woman's shoulders as she spoke in a sultry voice.

"We're inside the store now, and it's just like you'd figure it would be. They're even playing classic rock." She stuck her tongue out and flashed a devil's horns symbol with her hand. "Rock on! Here, let me show you around."

The woman slowly panned the camera toward the counter. Ned imagined her filming the entirety of the store. He wondered who she was making the video for. He backpedaled until he hit a cooler door.

"It's got everything you'd expect," the woman said. She pointed at a shelf. "Snacks, supplies, and beer. Beer!" The woman stepped onto the wet linoleum and slipped. "Whoa!"

Before she could fall, the nearby man caught her by the shoulders. The woman didn't drop her phone. She immediately lifted it over her face while she hovered parallel to the floor. "That was intense but so cool!"

"Wet floor," the man said. He lifted her upright.

The woman eyed the water and then moved the camera so it could record it. She squatted and pointed a finger at the floor. "Can you see that? It's so wet. Like totally sopping. A major hazard. Who's working in this joint?" The woman stood, and her eyes scanned the store.

Ned couldn't backpedal any further. His shoulders were pressed against the beer cooler.

"Hey, you," the woman said. "Do you work here?" She stepped forward carefully, and her companion remained watchfully behind. "That floor is dangerous." She pushed the phone toward Ned.

He pointed at the yellow sign. "It warned you."

"You believe this guy?" The woman spun the camera to herself. "I'm changing my opinion of this place." She eyed her companion. "Brick, what's the name of this joint?"

"Quik N Go."

"That's right," she said into her phone. "Brick and I are at the Eagle's Feet Quik N Go, and unless things turn around radically with this guy—" She spun the phone to Ned once more. "What's your name?"

He stared at her.

She turned the camera back to herself. "Whatever. If things don't turn around radically, I'm gonna tell you to avoid this place at all costs. Heck, maybe avoid all the Quik N Gos. Now, you know me—" She smiled in a righteous manner. "I'm a peaceable girl, and I like to give everyone a second chance and— No!" The woman's face pinched with anger. She lowered the phone and banged it against her free hand. "This can't be happening."

Ned cocked his head.

"What?" Brick asked.

"Not now!"

"Relax, Kiki."

"Don't tell me to relax." She looked up pleadingly. "I lost the stream."

"How?"

Kiki spread her arms. "How would I know?" She looked at her phone again. "Wait. I don't have service. Do you have it?"

Brick pulled his phone from a pocket. "None."

She wandered off. "Why does this always happen to me? What did I do?"

Ned eyed Brick.

The man motioned after Kiki. "She gets this way, but what can you do?"

"I don't know."

"Things must get pretty janky out here," Brick said, "especially with the weather." He faced the windows. "You hear about the roads? They're a yard sale."

"I'll bet."

Brick turned back to Ned. "They're so bad they closed the mountain. For real. We received a text alert." The guy consulted his phone, then lifted it so Ned could see. "I know, right? It totally sucks because Kiki and I are supposed to meet some guys for a review of a new snowmobile. Kiki on Kiki. Get it?"

The nearby mountain was the Walla Kiki so, yeah, Ned got it.

Kiki returned and stood next to Brick. Her face soured, and she shoved her phone in front of him. "This place is trash. What are we? Stuck in the eighteen hundreds or something?" She impatiently shook her cell phone. "How long does it take to get service back up?" She looked at Ned. "Do you have bars?"

"Not anywhere close, but Casper's got more

than a few."

She clucked her tongue. "What are you talking about?"

Ned realized then what she meant, and he shrugged off his misunderstanding. He had a cell phone, but it was a burner and intended for use in emergencies only. It was in his bungalow under the pillow on his bed. "Usually, we've got service, but it's never that great. Maybe we're in a pocket or something."

Brick tucked his phone away. "The blizzard must have knocked out a tower."

"How does that happen?" Kiki asked. "This is supposed to be Wyoming. Cowboy country. Don't they make things tougher out here?"

Overhead the song ended. *"Whoa! What a blast from the past with Winger! This is Headbanger Harv rocking you through the storm on Classic 106.9 FM."* The announcer's voice dropped an octave and grew serious. *"Returning to breaking news coverage. Due to a historic weather event, state law enforcement has shut down all highway traffic. Travelers are encouraged to find immediate housing or to shelter in place."*

"See?" Brick said. "What'd I tell you?"

Ned turned to the windows. Outside, the blizzard seemed to have intensified over the past thirty minutes.

"The storm is expected to last until the morning. Ski resort closures are coming in now. White Pine, Pine Creek, and Eagle's Feet have all closed their night skiing and may remain closed

tomorrow. Hogadon is expected to close any time now."

Kiki jiggled her phone and then lifted it high above her head. She grunted with frustration.

"In other news, police are still searching for those involved in the robbery of the Casper branch of the National Bank of Wyoming. The suspects are now believed to be driving westbound in a late model white Chevy van."

Kiki smacked her phone. She held it in the air again and touched the metal door jamb. "Ugh. What do I have to do?"

"There's been no detail on how much money the suspects got away with. Further information will be provided as it is made available." Headbanger Harv's voice perked up. *"I mean, like seriously, do these cops even try with this stuff?"* He rustled a paper near the microphone. *"What did they tell us? It's like they're purposefully trying to give us nothing. Well, let's forget them with the jamming beauties of Vixen!"*

Ned allowed his gaze to focus on the window reflections of the store's customers. "Were you needing something?"

"We saw your sign as we drove by. The one for the bungalows. We figured it was safer to stay here than push on any further."

Ned looked toward the pylon. Due to the heavy snowfall, he couldn't see the reader board from this distance. "How many rooms?"

"Just one." Brick stepped near the counter.

"Don't get your hopes up," Ned said. "They're pretty old."

"All we want to do is get off the road."

Kiki glanced up from her phone. "What's the Wi-Fi password?"

Ned moved toward the cash register. "We don't have Wi-Fi."

"What about the rooms?" Kiki asked. There was more than a hint of panic in her question.

"No Wi-Fi there, either."

Kiki faced Brick. "We can't stay here. We can't be disconnected."

"It'll be okay." He gently put his hands on her shoulders. "There's not a lot we can do in this storm."

"Yes, there is. We can keep driving."

Brick motioned toward the windows. "There's no visibility. It's not worth it."

"But the Kikinators need to know what I'm doing. My life is important to them."

"Your life is important to me, too."

Ned pulled out the registration book from under the counter. This would be the first time he used it. He flipped it open. The last time someone had stayed in a bungalow was more than a year ago. The book didn't seem that hard to fill out. When he reached for a pen, he asked, "What's a Kikinator?"

"My fiancée is an influencer," Brick said.

There were influencers in the Satan's Dawgs, too. They ran the club's protection rackets. This woman in her form-fitting ski outfit didn't look like one of them. Although, with the *Ride or Die* sticker in the back window of the truck, he suspected they both might be affiliated with the biker community.

"Brick's gonna be an influencer, too," she said, "if I have anything to do with it."

The man smiled indulgently. "I'm working on it, but it's clear who the guys like to watch more."

She shook her head. "They like to watch your stunts and stuff."

"It's okay. This is your thing."

Her attention returned to her phone. "We can't be disconnected, or they're gonna forget all about me." She quickly looked at Brick. "Us."

"Not for one night," Brick said. "Everything will be okay."

Ned asked, "Names?"

"Brighton Bennington," the man said. "And yeah, it's real."

"That's why we call him Brick," Kiki said. "It trends better."

Brick pulled a wallet from a pocket, then removed his driver's license and handed it to Ned.

He read it out loud. "Brighton Byron Bennington. Your childhood must have been rough."

"I grew up in Connecticut, so it worked in my favor. But Kiki is right. The name isn't good for what we're doing."

"Which is?"

"A video channel dedicated to reviewing bikes and snowmobiles."

Ned straightened. His earlier unease seemed warranted now. "What kind of bikes?"

"Motocross. You know the kind?"

"Dirt bikes."

"Right. Kiki got into them because of me, and now she's developed a huge following." He chuckled. "It's not rocket science. Some guys like watching girls talk about motorcycles. Go figure."

Ned looked down to hide his concerns. He set Brick's driver's license on the counter and then entered the man's information into the registry. He lived in Moab, Utah. When he was done, he pushed the card back. Ned announced the room rate.

"If you're interested, you can check out her stuff. Just type in Kiki Ziegler. You can't miss her."

Kiki tapped her phone and held it away from her and slightly above her head. She looked up at it and said, "Hey-ho, Kikinators! Okay, so we lost the stream, but as they say, adapt and overcome. This will take off from where the stream so abruptly ended. Brick and I are checking into a bungalow at—" Her face pinched, and she flipped the phone toward Ned. "What's the name of this business again?"

Brick said, "Quik N Go."

She turned the camera around and held it above her. "That's right! We're at the Eagle's Feet Quik N Go." Kiki announced this flamboyantly like a ringmaster calling a show to start. Immediately, her face scrunched. "But it's not as exciting as it sounds. We lost cell service, which was sketchy to begin with, and now there's no Wi-Fi at this station. It's not a four-star destination because of that alone." Kiki wandered through the store and continued talking to her phone.

Brick tucked his driver's license into his wallet before pulling out a credit card. He set it on the counter.

"I thought the cell service was out," Ned said.

"Probably still is. Kiki's recording some content onto her phone so we can upload later when the towers come back online."

Ned started the credit card machine.

"What about that thing?" Brick said. "It's going to work?"

"Landline." Ned pulled the small machine away from the wall to reveal a cord. He typed in the amount owed and inserted Brick's credit card. "What was she doing when you guys walked in? If she can film now, why'd she get so upset?"

"She was livestreaming."

Ned didn't like the sound of that.

"It's like broadcast TV but straight to her channel. You'd be surprised how many guys tune in to watch her." Brick watched his fiancée. "For whatever reason, they go crazy when she goes live."

While the machine processed the credit card transaction, Ned eyed Kiki. She continued talking into her phone as she picked up various items. She held them for the camera to see.

When the machine dinged its acceptance, Ned removed the card and set it on the counter.

He then pulled a room key from the board behind him.

Kiki sat on the beer display with her legs kicked out in front of her. She continued to film herself as she talked.

"Which one is ours?" Brick asked.

"Two," Ned said. "It's around back. I'll take you there."

He grabbed his red winter coat from the chair and slipped an arm into it. Travis sat upright and stretched.

Brick called over his shoulder. "We're ready, Kiki. Let's go."

"These Kikinators," Ned said, "they're what exactly?"

"Her fans." Brick must have noticed Ned's souring disposition. "On her social media platforms."

Even though he knew what Brick meant, he muttered another expletive. "Followers."

Kiki backpedaled toward them as she continued to record herself. Brick waved at the camera. Ned scooped up the cat and walked toward the end of the counter.

"Not just any followers," Brick said, "she's totally branded them. Kiki is a marketing genius."

"How many are there?"

Kiki stopped at the counter now. "From the Quik N Go in Eagle's Feet—" She smiled and flashed a peace sign. "—this is Kiki and Brick and—" she turned the phone toward Ned and the cat. "Aw, look it. What a cute boy. What's its name?" She held the camera near Travis, which also highlighted the tattoo on the back of Ned's right hand.

He muttered, "You can pick."

It was a stupid thing to say. When he first met the cat, it was in the mystery bookstore in Maine. Visitors to the store were allowed to call the tom anything they wanted as long as it was a mystery protagonist. Ned tried to carry on the naming rule when he moved, but the convention didn't stick. Besides, Ned liked the name he gave the cat.

Yet, he just dumbly uttered the old naming rule. He was the former bookkeeper of the Satan's Dawgs, for crying out loud. How could a social media maven with her cell phone camera make him nervous? Why couldn't people just live their lives without pulling out a phone every few seconds?

Kiki whipped the camera back to herself and bugged her eyes. "What did he say?" She grinned widely. "I can pick its name?" She spun the phone back to Ned. "You're gonna need to explain that."

"Never mind," Ned said. "His name is Travis."

"No," Kiki said. "You said I get to pick." She turned the camera back to herself. "And if I get to pick a cat's name, it would be something magnificent." Kiki touched a finger to her chin as if lost in thought. "Cheddar Sprocket!" Her eyes bulged for the phone. "What do you think? Hit the like button if you agree!"

Ned stepped around her. "It's Travis."

Kiki clucked her tongue. "Travis sounds like the color of my grandfather's shoes."

He faced her and found himself staring directly into the camera. "Turn that off."

She barked a laugh. "Whatevs." Kiki looked once more into the phone. "A million Kikinators will make a guy nervous." She winked, kissed her fingers, then wriggled them. "Peace out, boys and girls. Always remember, you're either slicing the wind or you're eating dust. Where do you want to be?"

After a final smooch to the screen, Kiki stopped recording. The smile faded from her face. "At least we can upload something when we get signal again."

Brick gently grabbed her arm and pulled her toward the door. "He's going to walk us to the room."

"It better be nice," she said. "I hate doing negative content."

"*Kiki,*" Brick said.

"What? The fans want to know where we stayed. If it's not nice, I need to warn them. It's my duty." She eyed Ned. "I could have made you and Cheddar Sprocket famous." Her gaze swept over the store. "Well, sort of famous, but don't be surprised if people start showing up here to see that adorable boy."

Ned frowned. Her livestream and subsequent video were going to be a problem.

He grabbed a sign from the counter and hung it on the glass door. It read *Back in Five Minutes.* Then he pushed the door open. Brick and Kiki stepped past him into the gusting snow.

Travis buried his head into Ned's chest.

"Meet at the second bungalow." He walked off without waiting for them to reply.

Chapter 5

Ned lowered his head as he pushed forward into the gusting snow. He did his best to protect the cat from the wind. More than a foot of powder had accumulated on the sidewalk.

He plodded through the snow around the rear. It was much darker back there. Only one light fixture hung on the rear of the Quik N Go. Each of the bungalows had a single bulb affixed near its front door.

Ned trudged toward the first structure. Parked near it was a thirty-year-old pickup with a snowplow blade attached to its front. After the snow let up, Ned would use the four-wheel-drive truck to clear the store's parking lot. He'd already used it once since he arrived. When he first saw the pickup and its blade, he mistakenly thought it would be fun to operate. Pushing snow around a parking lot didn't give him the type of thrill he'd imagined. Truth be told, not much did at Eagle's Feet.

After Ned opened the door to his bungalow, Travis jumped from his arm and shook. Snow flew from his body.

Ned took a moment to check the cell phone tucked under his pillow. It was an old-style flip phone with no numbers programmed into it. Ned was disciplined enough not to enter any information into a phone. If he ever lost it or it was taken from him, no one would get anything from it.

He opened the phone to confirm what Brick and Kiki had said—there was currently no cell service in the area. The blizzard must have somehow been responsible.

Was there only one cell tower in the area? Was there not a redundant system in place? Ned didn't know the intricacies of a cellular network, nor did he care to learn. There was a landline inside the store, and that provided him with all the telephone access he would need.

He slipped the phone back under the pillow.

"Stay warm," he said to the cat.

Ned didn't bother locking the door after he pulled it closed. No one had rented a bungalow before tonight, and if someone decided to sneak around back here, Ned would see them.

Besides, he didn't have much to steal. A couple of books, a knitting kit, a cat carrier, and Travis. And if someone decided to steal his cat...

Well, Ned reluctantly admitted he'd probably miss the darn thing.

He clomped through the snow toward the second bungalow. Each unit was roughly fifty feet apart. Ned thought the distance was excessive, but it was Wyoming, and there was plenty of space for it.

His thoughts drifted to Kiki Ziegler and her cell phone camera. She'd invaded his privacy and created a dilemma for him, but did that mean danger from it was a sure thing? And would he have more trouble if she posted the second video?

Being shown on social media was why Ned had to flee Costa Buena, California, where he'd gone by the alias of Owen Hunter. "Owen" had gotten into a couple of altercations that were filmed by bystanders.

The first was with some local skate hoodlums. Onlookers recorded him and posted it on the internet. He had no idea where the videos went—that's what the girls who hung around the Satan's Dawgs were for. They knew where to find that kind of stuff.

He probably would have been okay with just the fight videos, but what caused Ned's former identity real trouble was when he made the evening news for crossing a group of gray-haired political activists. They alerted the television stations who splashed his picture all over the airwaves.

That brought the Dawgs.

So, just how badly would Kiki Ziegler's video affect him? He decided it depended on who saw it. Indeed some had already seen her livestream, but did that stay around forever? He didn't know as he'd never watched one. Could someone watch a livestream whenever they wanted? Was it possible to delete a livestream, and if so, could Ned convince Kiki to delete it along with the other video she recorded?

A pair of headlights bounced their way around the back and passed Ned. The Ford Raptor pulled in front of the second bungalow and stopped.

Ned walked by the truck and unlocked the unit. He swung the door open and stepped inside. Everything was clean—he'd made sure of that himself. Ned took pride in his work. However, there was only so much a vacuum and cleaning products could do.

While the sheets and bedspread were washed, they were still old—possibly decades. Ned's grandmother had very old bedding, but it always smelled of her house—slightly musty and a little like cookies. It was a difficult aroma to describe, but he missed it. These fabrics didn't smell like that, and Ned had cleaned them with the large washing machine located in the main building's storeroom.

Ned had also vacuumed the worn beige carpet a couple of times, but there was no way to get rid of the wear patterns.

He wasn't a neat freak—far from it. He'd simply been bored over the past several weeks. No one cared if he closed the convenience store for an hour or two and cleaned. Travelers could still stop and get gas, paying at the pumps. That's what most of them did anyway.

If the guys in the club ever heard how he'd spent hours cleaning to avoid boredom, they would have kicked him out of the club. Dawgs didn't scrub, do dishes, or wash their clothes. They got others to do those tasks for them. For a while, Ned thought that was an acceptable way of life. Now, he knew it wasn't.

When Brick and Kiki stepped inside the bungalow, she gasped.

Ned shut the door behind the couple. "As I said, it's a little dated."

"This is," Kiki stammered, "the most—"

Brick lifted his hands. "It's only one night."

"—horrid place—" she covered her mouth, "I've ever seen."

"We'll be out first thing," Brick said. "As soon as the storm breaks."

Kiki dropped her bag and touched the wall with her fingers. "Is that real wood paneling? Oh, my God. That's wood paneling!" She spun around. "Are we in the *Twilight Zone*? What year is it?"

Brick rubbed her back. "Everything is fine."

She pointed at the telephone on the nightstand. "Does that work?" She lifted the handset and put it to her ear. Her eyes widened. "No way. Stop it." Kiki shoved the receiver toward Brick. "Do you hear that? This thing works. Who should we call? Who was alive in 1975?"

"If you have any issues," Ned said, "pound zero will call the store."

Kiki's brow furrowed. "Pound?" She looked at Brick. "What's a pound?"

Ned pointed at the symbol on the telephone.

Kiki inhaled sharply. "A hashtag! They had hashtags on phones back then?"

Brick gently touched her fingers and pushed the handset back into place.

"Pound one," Ned said, "will get you to my bungalow."

She clapped. "Pound! Oh my God, wait till I

tell the Kikinators. Let's get set up." She lifted her hands and held her two thumbs together. She spun around the room. "We'll shoot this direction."

"About your video—" Ned said.

Kiki moved her two hands until she was staring through a small pair of goalposts at him.

"The one you made in the store."

"What about it?" Suspicion filled her voice.

"Any chance you would delete it?"

"Why would I do that?"

Brick moved next to her. "Yeah. Why would she do that?"

"It's just—" Ned frowned. "I don't want to be on camera."

Kiki put her hands on her hips. "Are you going to make this difficult?"

His former self—the bookkeeper—most certainly would have made it difficult. He would have taken the woman's phone and destroyed it. Had she or the boyfriend tried to stop him, well, they would have been dealt with accordingly. They weren't professionals, so it wouldn't have risen to the level of permanent harm. A hard slap would likely get the job done with her. The guy might have needed a solid punch to the belly to bring things into focus. However, Ned was no longer that man.

Brick asked, "Why don't you want to be on camera?"

"Family issues." It seemed like an easy, noncommittal answer. "That's why I work here."

"In the middle of nowhere," Brick said.

"I don't want my—" Ned paused to find the word. "—family to find me."

Brick cocked his head. "Are you running from the law?"

"No. The law knows exactly where I'm at."

Kiki studied her boyfriend. "What are you doing?"

"I'm asking the guy some questions."

"Well, stop." She leaned toward Ned. "I have lawyers, you know."

He nodded. "I'm sure."

"You can't make me delete anything I don't want."

"I understand."

"I've gone against tougher guys than you."

He doubted that, but Ned said, "Okay."

She eyed Brick as doubt flashed over her face. "What did we say? Did we say anything?"

"We said the company name."

Kiki rolled her eyes. "Big deal. I said where we were. I'd be willing to bleep that out but look at this place." She waved her arm around the room. "We have to tell my followers. We're allowed to say a company's name if we review the conditions." Her gaze returned to Ned. "So, no. I'm not going to delete it."

If she wouldn't get rid of the video, there was no way he could approach her about deleting the livestream—if such a thing was even possible.

Brick looked at Ned. "Don't worry about it, man. Her followers are mostly dudes. They won't bother you."

Kiki clucked her tongue. "My demographics are so much deeper than that. I'm totally trending older female now."

"I know, babe. I'm just saying."

"Don't placate me. You're not seriously suggesting I delete it."

"Of course not." Brick dismissively waved his hand. "But we could go back to the store and reshoot. I'll bring my camera. We'll frame it better. Make sure the lighting is just so." He made the okay sign with his thumb and index finger. "We can get the cat in more of the shots."

Her eyes widened with excitement. "Cheddar Sprocket."

"Right," Brick said. "We'll get Cheddar Sprocket and do something original. You know how the Kikinators love to see you with animals. Remember that one we did with the pugs?"

A small smile hinted at the edges of Kiki's lips. She glanced at Ned's hands. "Where's the cat?"

"Travis is home for the night."

"It's Cheddar Sprocket. You said I could name him." Her face pinched. "And for your info, I wouldn't name a dead squirrel after Kourtney K's husband."

Ned had no idea who Kourtney K was, what was wrong with her husband, or why Kiki would consider naming a dead squirrel anything.

She reappraised Ned. "Maybe you're right." She thumbed toward Ned. "I don't think he's going to go over well with our demos. He's too old and too... something."

"I don't know," Brick said. "I think he would look all right on a bike." To Ned, he asked. "You ever ride?"

Ned shook his head. It felt strange to lie about something he loved.

"See?" Kiki said. "I told you he's something. Let's plan to reshoot the whole thing."

Brick nodded knowingly. "Why don't I script up some talking points? Then we'll go back over later. Won't take but thirty minutes. How's that sound?"

Kiki sat on the edge of the bed. "Maybe you can make me a yogurt parfait first? My blood sugar's super low. I think I might faint." She dramatically flopped backward onto the bed.

Brick turned to Ned. "We'll come over later. We'll make sure you're not in the new footage. How's that sound?"

Ned nodded. "I'd appreciate that." He opened the door and stepped out into the howling wind.

Kiki yelled toward the ceiling, "And bring Cheddar Sprocket! I'm gonna make him a star!"

He pulled the door shut behind him. Ned lowered his head into the blowing snow. He wanted to believe that things would work out fine, but he knew better. Life rarely worked out the way he wanted. He needed to prepare for Kiki's eventual changing of her mind. She seemed the type to do such a thing.

His boots crunched into the accumulating snow, and his thoughts returned to the Satan's Dawgs.

The guys in his old club weren't sharp when

it came to technology. Whenever a computer was involved, they assigned the task to a prospect or one of the girls who hung around. The prospects weren't much better on the computer than the club's members, but it was part of their initiation. The Dawgs wouldn't have wanted some nerd in their ranks—being book smart was seen as a weakness. Only street smarts mattered.

When Ned returned to the front of the convenience store, he looked beyond the gas pumps. He couldn't see anything else through the darkness and the falling snow. He looked up into the night sky and blinked as flakes landed on his face. Ned brushed the powder from his cheeks and considered the sidewalk. The snow was much higher than his ankle. He reached inside the store, grabbed the shovel, and set to clearing the concrete. Unfortunately, there were so many footprints in the snow now that it wasn't going to be a clean walk. It didn't matter. He'd get off as much as possible.

And he wasn't doing it because that earlier fancy-pants customer complained. He was doing it for some exercise. And he wanted to keep his mind busy.

As much as he hated admitting it, he worried about Kiki Ziegler. He didn't understand social media well enough to comprehend its reach. Maybe the Dawgs *would* find him because of her videos. He had no idea if any of the girls who hung around the Dawgs considered themselves Kikinators. And maybe some of the guys watched the videos, too.

Ned also had to worry about the mafia. He had crossed a regional gangster while living in Maine. That's when he learned just how truly connected the mob was worldwide. His name was added to a database of informants hiding in the witness protection program. Ned knew of its existence because he'd seen it— www.thefbiisabunchofdirtyrats.com.

The people hunting for him were much larger than a group of outlaw bikers from Phoenix, Arizona. The criminal network looking for FBI rats was well-funded and highly organized. Anyone of them could be a fan of Kiki Ziegler.

Ned finished shoveling and banged the blade against the sidewalk to clear away the chunks of snow clinging to it. When he returned to the store, he put the shovel near the front door.

From the speakers overhead, a poppy, hair metal song wound down. *"Welcome back, dudes and dudettes. This is Headbanger Harv on Classic 106.9 FM. You just heard Babylon A.D. with 'Bang Go the Bells.'"*

Ned stood on the mat and stomped the snow from his feet. He removed his coat and brushed the remaining powder from it.

Headbanger Harv cheerfully continued. *"Man, I miss the eighties. It seems all anyone ever wants to sing about now are feelings. What's that all about? Did we time warp back to the seventies? I'll pass. They can keep that touchy-feely disco nonsense to themselves, thank you very much."*

Ned pulled the *Around Back* sign from the door and headed toward the counter.

The announcer's voice became grave. *"Returning to the breaking news story we've been following all night. Authorities have no new information following the robbery of the National Bank of Wyoming in Casper. They are still tallying the amount of money stolen. According to law enforcement officials, tonight's historic blizzard is hampering their pursuit."*

Ned pulled the telephone to him. He should alert the marshals to Kiki Ziegler's livestream video. Maybe she would keep her word and never upload the second one. But if she did, perhaps he could stop that one from ever being seen. The marshals could do that, right?

"The suspects wore masks during the robbery, so there are no physical descriptions of the individuals involved. Officials believe there were five men who fled the scene together in a white Chevy van. Extreme caution is advised. Again, extreme caution is advised."

Ned bounced his finger across the phone pad. It was a number he'd committed to memory. He was about to press the last button when a set of headlights pierced the night sky.

"Wow," Headbanger Harv said, *"they sure made that sound scary!"* He chuckled. *"I wouldn't want to get caught alone with one of those guys. Let's lighten things up with Poison's 'Look What the Cat Dragged In.'"*

As the vehicle approached, Ned set the receiver down. He straightened and crossed his arms.

A white Chevy van slid to a stop at the front of the store. It hit the concrete bumper, and the vehicle bounced once. Its headlights snapped off, and several faces peered into the store.

Chapter 6

The side door of the Chevy van slid open as the driver calmly exited his seat. A tall white woman emerged from the passenger's seat. Three white men hopped from the interior of the van. There was a chubby one, a skinny one, and one who looked so boringly normal that Ned faltered on the way to describe him.

All who exited the van wore the same outfit—black knit caps, puffy black coats, blue jeans, and black boots. None held anything in their hands.

Inside the store, Ned rested his elbows on the counter. There was nothing to do but bide his time. He knew what was coming, and getting worried was a waste of energy. It was better to remain calm and wait for this new batch of customers to enter the store.

Perhaps he should have finished his phone call. He had intended to dial the emergency hotline that the U.S. Marshals established for him. They would have immediately traced the call to this location if they had answered. That was the standard procedure. If Ned had hung up right after a connection was made, they still might have traced the call. Surely, they would try to call him back. If he didn't answer, perhaps they would send someone to investigate. Would it have been Goodspeed or another agent? No, more than likely, they would have sent a local law enforcement officer.

None of that mattered now because Ned didn't press the final number to complete the call. He suspected who these customers were, and he didn't want any law enforcement to arrive. He might desire to be a better man, but that didn't mean he enjoyed being a rat. The cops could stay right where they were.

Ned considered the new arrivals as they lingered outside near their van. Maybe this crew only needed some gas. Yet, why weren't they next to a pump if that were the case? He quickly tossed that theory away.

The driver was a white man in his late fifties, and his face held a stony resolve. He pulled his shoulders back and stood straight with what appeared to be a commanding presence.

The passengers must have felt some loyalty as they watched the driver with a sort of anxiety. He never bothered to look at any of them, though. Instead, his gaze remained focused on the darkness beyond the edge of the convenience store's parking lot. The driver muttered something, and the others turned away with some humiliation. Each scanned the outer darkness with a similar intensity as their leader.

Maybe what Ned had first thought of as loyalty was instead fear. Ned knew that loyalty and fear existed in every organization. A soldier's dedication wasn't always due to a higher calling. Sometimes anxiety at a superior's punishment could get a soldier to act. That was definitely the culture inside the Satan's Dawgs—some were dedicated to the cause while others were dedicated to avoiding punishment. Ned imagined corporate employees might subscribe to something similar. Therefore, why would it be so different for the group of five outside?

Ned stopped considering loyalty and fear to return to pondering this crew's reason for being at the Quik N Go. Perhaps, they needed a restroom. If that were the case, they'd be sorely disappointed. He'd send them down the road, though probably without jerking them around like he had the last guy who'd asked. But send them where? The blizzard made travel difficult. They couldn't go back to Casper without the cops looking for them. Since the state patrol had closed the highway, did that mean there were roadblocks with troopers staffing them? That seemed unlikely. There couldn't be many officers available, and would the state risk a trooper in the cold for that long? Again, that was doubtful.

Perhaps road closures were done by the honor system. He didn't know as he'd never been in a state that had done such a thing. Maybe the government announced that drivers must remain off a highway and simply expected its citizens to comply. Only a gullible resident would do so.

Ned raised an eyebrow as a gust of wind blew the heavy snowfall sideways.

Maybe some less-than-naive travelers would comply with the state order tonight. But Evanston was only an hour away. This crew should be able to make it that far, even in this blizzard. It would take persistence and careful driving, but they could surely do it if they wanted. Stopping at the Quik N Go while being pursued seemed an unnecessary risk.

Were the roads that bad?

Outside, the driver turned as if on a rotisserie. With repeated small steps, his body moved but his head never did. Eventually, his gaze passed by the store windows. When his eyes landed on Ned, the driver briefly paused his shuffling.

Ned did what he assumed a citizen would. He forced an awkward smile and lifted a hand in a friendly gesture. "I feel stupid," he said through clenched teeth.

The driver cocked his head.

Even though the gesture felt foolish, Ned was sure he'd done the right thing. Citizens did silly things that often boggled him. He broadened his fake grin and waved like a kid at a passing train.

The driver frowned before continuing his scan.

Ned's smile melted, and his expression returned to its natural state.

When the driver completed a full turn, he shut his door and stepped onto the sidewalk. The female passenger spun, grabbed her door, and slammed it closed. The chubby man violently yanked the sliding door shut. The group reassembled on the sidewalk but didn't move toward the front door.

Once more, the driver searched the darkness stretching out along the highway. The others eyed each other with some unspoken skepticism. Then they slowly turned away from one another to study the perimeter.

Ned scratched his cheek. Perhaps this crew needed traveling snacks. Customers occasionally dropped in for that exact reason. They'd zip into the parking lot, run into the store for a bag of chips and a soda, then hit the road again. Ned never did that while with the Dawgs. Holding a handful of goodies while guiding a motorcycle down the freeway was doable, but it wasn't cool enough to outweigh the risks.

No, he finally decided—this crew was not here for snacks. A blizzard didn't seem the time for munchies. It was time for everyone to pay attention to the road.

When the driver was satisfied with his scan of the horizon, he nodded once and said something. This brought visible sighs of relief from several of the crew. They moved as a group toward the front door.

Overhead, the doorbell warbled ominously against the radio's latest offering.

The driver stopped on the mat, and the others shuffled awkwardly past him like water moving around a rock.

None of the crew bothered to stamp the snow from their boots nor wipe it from their coats, yet all of them eyed Ned. The chubby one and the woman showed no fear. However, the skinny man and the boringly normal one seemed almost apologetic for their entrance.

Ned straightened and motioned toward the window. "Some storm, huh? How bad are the roads?"

He didn't care about the highway. It was simply a topic that most people liked to chat about when they entered the store. Even in the short time he'd been at the Quik N Go, he'd divided the customers into two camps. Some complained about how much worse the Wyoming highways were than those 'back home,' and then there were those customers who complimented the Cowboy State's roads when compared to those in their home state.

Ned figured the friendly questions might put everyone at ease.

The driver pulled open his coat to reveal a wooden-handled revolver tucked into his waistband. Another gun hung under his left armpit—this one seemed much larger and appeared to be an automatic.

Maybe this crew didn't speak English, Ned thought. Therefore, he spoke clearly and carefully enunciated every word, "Can I help you find something?"

The driver's face darkened, and he let his coat fall closed. "Ringo," he said.

Ned had heard the word before, but it seemed a strange thing for the man to utter. Perhaps it was a threat in a foreign language. Or maybe Ringo was a greeting. But in what language?

German? Russian? Ned hadn't detected an accent. Could a person reveal their country's origin in such a simple word? He didn't know.

So, Ned lifted his hand and said, "Ringo."

The woman moved next to the driver. She appeared to be in her mid-thirties. Tufts of blond hair peeked out from beneath her black beanie. She seemed irritated by Ned merely being in the store.

"What's his problem?" she asked. A southern drawl filled those two words. "You think he knows—"

Ned lowered his hand. Ringo did not mean hello.

"Take the back," the driver said.

Her expression flattened, and she faced the driver. "Yeah, sure, but this one—" she thumbed at Ned, "he doesn't look right." She glanced at the others. "I can't be the only one that thinks that, right?"

"Ringo," the driver said.

She lifted her hands in surrender. "All right, all right. No need to raise your voice." She ambled toward the back of the store. "I was just commenting on the big fella. You don't have to make it a federal offense." She chuckled and looked back over her shoulder. "That's pretty funny, huh?"

"Ringo!"

"What?" she hollered.

"Stop talking."

Ned pointed toward the restroom. "It's out."

The driver's brow furrowed. "What's out?"

"The toilet—it's broken." Ned mimed the act of flushing.

At the restroom door, Ringo wiggled the knob. "It's locked."

"Because it's broken," Ned called. "Like I said."

Anger flashed on the chubby man's face, and he stepped toward Ned. The driver grabbed his shoulder to stop him.

"Aw, c'mon," the chubby man said, "Let me smack him around."

"No."

"Just a little."

The driver shook his head. "You see the size of him, Paul?"

Paul put his hand under his coat. "I'll take care of him."

"No," the driver said.

"Why not?"

"Because I said so."

Paul clucked his tongue. "Just when I thought we were starting to have some fun." He stepped back, but his eyes narrowed when he was out of the driver's line of sight. Paul watched Ned with open hostility.

"Ringo," the driver said. "Stay where you are."

"Roger that." The woman stepped away from the restroom door and looked to the front of the store. "But if no one is in there, how come I gotta hang out back here? This feels like a punishment."

"Ringo."

"Why won't you ever answer a straight

question?" she said. "Are you mad at me or something? What'd I do?"

"Stop talking."

Ringo's lips pursed, and she kicked the bottom of the bathroom door. It rattled loudly throughout the store. "Sorry. I slipped."

"George," the driver said.

The boringly normal man shuffled forward. He was in his early forties. He stood almost six feet tall with medium shoulders. "Yeah?"

"Check the stockroom."

George glanced over his shoulder to a room marked to hold extra goods. "Right."

"You're not going to get much," Ned said. "Chips and candy, maybe. Plus a washer and dryer."

"Can it," the driver said. His eyes shifted to George. "What are you waiting for? Get a move on."

The boring man sighed and stuck his hand inside his coat. He moved toward the stockroom. He opened the door and peeked his head in.

"Get going, you big baby," Ringo said.

George stepped inside and the door shut behind him.

"Why do we gotta have him with us?" Paul asked.

"Zip it," the driver said. "Both of you."

"The cigarettes are in there," Ned said. "They could probably fetch a few bucks."

The driver faced Ned. "What part of 'can it,' aren't you understanding?"

Ned pointed at the stockroom. "If you're gonna rob the joint, I figured you'd want to know where the valuable stuff was at."

"The only thing I want to know is if someone else is in the store."

"I could have told you that."

The driver cocked his head. "Maybe we don't trust you."

George stepped out of the stockroom and shrugged.

"What's that?" the driver asked with an exaggerated shrug. "I don't understand what that means."

"It means nobody's in there."

"Geez," Ringo said, "nice attitude."

George smirked. "Mind your own business."

Ringo glared at him. "After all he did for us? You might show a little enthusiasm for this job."

"Ringo," the driver said.

She faced him. "What'd I do now?"

"Stop talking."

"But I was defending you."

The driver snapped his fingers in front of the tall man's face. "John, wake up."

John must have been six foot five and nearly forty years old. He'd been staring at Ned. Even though his gaze now settled on the driver, he remained silent.

"The cooler," the driver said.

The tall man nodded once, then eyed Ned again.

"Now."

John entered the cooler. He didn't reach for

anything hidden inside his coat before going inside.

Ned opened his mouth to speak, but the driver angrily pointed at him. "I know what's inside a cooler."

"There's a freezer in there, too."

The driver's lips pinched. "What'd I say?"

"Maybe there's an aftermarket for Hot Pockets. I don't know. You can take some. We have a good stock of them."

"Keep your comments to yourself."

For several seconds, John was out of sight. He soon reappeared and shrugged a single shoulder.

"You're as bad as him." The driver motioned toward George. "Is it clear?"

He nodded.

"Then say so."

John crossed his arms. "Clear."

"Was that so hard?"

The driver leaned toward Paul. "Stay here and keep a watch."

Paul nodded. He was the youngest of the group, but not by much. Ned guessed him to be roughly thirty years old. The guy faced the windows and scanned the snowy darkness. He seemed the most enthusiastic of the bunch, even more so than the woman.

The driver proceeded to the front counter. The skin crinkled at the edges of his steel blue eyes. "Where's Kenny?"

"Who?"

"Kenny Piersee." The driver tapped the

counter. "He works here."

"I'm the only guy working here. The boss is supposed to hire someone new, but right now, it's just me. Makes for some long days, but I don't mind."

The driver emphatically tapped the counter again. "Kenny works here. Or he did."

Ned shrugged. "If you say so. I got the job after some guy died."

The driver cocked his head. "Kenny died?"

"If that's his name."

"How'd it happen?"

"Heart attack from what I was told. Guess it happened over there near the door." He pointed to where Paul stood looking out the window.

Paul looked down at the floor mat and stepped back several feet.

"You sure like to talk," the driver said.

Ned didn't usually like to talk. He was simply chatting while he formed a plan. Unfortunately, one wasn't coming quickly to him, so he continued to speak. "It's quiet around here, so I get sort of friendly when someone shows up."

"That's not it." The driver tugged the gun free from his waistband and set it on the counter. His right hand covered it.

Ned tapped a button on the register, and the drawer popped open. "It's been a slow night on account of the weather, but you're welcome to whatever I've got. There's nothing in the safe." He motioned toward the floor. "You're free to look if you want."

"That's kind of you."

"Help yourself to some snacks, too." Ned reached past the driver's gun and over the counter. He grabbed a box of Mike & Ike's from the front shelf. "We're running a special on these—two for one. They delivered too many, so we've got to move them."

The driver stared at him.

"Take as many as you like."

The driver slipped the Mike & Ike's from Ned's hand and carefully set them back in the shelf. "You don't belong here."

"Sure, I do."

The driver shook his head. "Everything about you is wrong."

"That's what I said," Ringo called out.

Ned motioned toward the shelf. "If you don't like candy, there's also a special on peanuts." He considered the others in the store. "Any of you have nut allergies?"

"We don't want snacks," the driver said. "How long have you been here?"

"Three weeks."

The driver scratched his cheek with the barrel of his gun. "Kenny died three weeks ago?"

Ned shrugged a single shoulder. "Thereabouts. I never met the man."

"Where were you before?"

"In the Coast Guard." The lie was part of the cover that Ned memorized before arriving in Wyoming.

Each member of the crew looked at him. He expected them to thank him for his service. That happened to him previously when he'd claimed he was a member of the Navy. However, Ned didn't think that was going to happen now. The crew's faces scrunched in emotions ranging from shock to disbelief.

"The Coast Guard?" the driver asked. "What were you doing there?"

"I was a mechanic."

Paul pointed at Ned. "Why are we wasting our time with this guy?"

The driver lifted a hand. "Did you fix boats?"

"Cars and trucks, mostly. How else are coasties going to get around?"

"Coasties?"

"Guardsmen," Ned said.

The driver studied him. "This is a little far from the water. What brought you here?"

"A girl." It was another lie that Marshal Goodspeed created for his cover.

Revealing a fictional love interest brought a collective "ah" from the other crew members except for Paul. The driver looked over his shoulder and scowled.

Paul pointed at himself. "What? I didn't do that."

"Me neither," Ringo said. "I was only yawning." She opened her mouth and stretched her arms in the air. She pointed a finger at John. "It was him."

The driver turned back to Ned. "And where is this girl now?"

"She ran off with a skier." As an afterthought, he added, "An instructor from the resort."

There was a second round of "ahs," but these

were filled with remorse.

"I'm not buying it," the driver said.

Ringo clapped her hands in the air. "Me neither. Just so you know."

"What's to buy?" Ned asked. "She wasn't your girl."

The driver leaned in, and he scowled. "I know what this place is."

"It's a gas station." Ned spread his arms apart. "So, are you robbing this joint or what?"

The driver straightened. After several moments of consideration, he said, "We need rooms." He lifted the gun and waggled it

Ned did his best to hide his disappointment. First, the social media influencer showed up and filmed him, and now this crew. He should have called the marshals and left the phone line open.

The driver's eyes narrowed. "I'm watching you."

"I know," Ned said, "that's why I'm including the cable TV for free."

Chapter 7

Overhead, a new song started, and it was another Ned hadn't heard before. Anxious guitars and sprightly drum play backed a lead singer who yowled like a cat. A lyric had yet to be sung. Ned suspected this was the best part of the song.

He cleared his throat. "How many rooms?"

"Two," the driver said. His gaze dropped to the fireball tattoo on the back of Ned's right hand. "Where'd you get the ink?"

"Seattle."

"Uh-huh." The driver sounded unconvinced. His eyes slowly returned to meet Ned's. Suspicion filled his voice. "Looks like a prison tattoo."

"Definitely not," Ned muttered.

The intense interest from the driver bothered Ned. Had he not been working to be a better man, he might have reached for the gun right there and then. The driver was sloppy with the revolver, waving it as he spoke and sometimes allowing it to get too close to Ned.

However, if Ned did snatch the gun from this man, it would likely lead to one thing—shooting everyone in the store. He wouldn't imagine that they would all lay down their weapons and go without a fight. A Wyoming bloodbath was something he'd like to avoid.

But perhaps the driver baited him by waving the gun about. Maybe it was feigned carelessness. If that were the case, then the driver wanted Ned to act. He had the cold, calculating eyes of a cop and the questions of one, too.

The man's inquiry into the whereabouts of Kenny Piersee concerned Ned. If Kenny was indeed in the witness protection program, had the driver come to connect with him? Had they planned some sort of reunion that now fell apart due to his death?

Ned reached for the register book and froze in mid-grab. "I need to get something from under here."

The driver's eyes narrowed. "Why tell me?"

"I'd like us on the same page." Ned looked beyond the driver to the members of his crew. Paul and Ringo had their hands underneath their coats, and suspicion filled their eyes. John and George simply watched him with curiosity. "I don't want any misinterpretations."

"That's very understanding of you," the driver said. He glanced back at his crew and motioned for them to relax. When he faced Ned again, he forced a joyless smile. "We'd like to avoid misinterpreting your actions as well."

Ned pulled the register from underneath the counter. Using it was futile—he knew that, but he still needed time to develop a plan. Completing the book's registration fields might buy him some.

Admittedly, things looked bad.

He was stuck in the middle of nowhere and locked in place by an active blizzard.

And Ned regretted passing on the opportunity to call for help. He had decided not to phone the marshals so he wouldn't be a rat. What outcome did he hope would happen?

The crew wanted to spend the night in the bungalows, which meant five wild cards were now in his orbit. If the storm continued longer, would they stay a second night? Or perhaps a third?

Ned mentally chastised himself for not calling the marshals. Being labeled a rat was terrible, but it was far preferable to being shot, killed, or killing someone.

He grabbed the corner of the register book and flipped it open. What Ned needed to do now was get the crew out of the store so he'd get another chance to call. He pulled a pen from a nearby container. "Driver's license?"

"Get serious," the driver said.

"I'm gonna need a name."

"Why?"

He pointed at the register book. "Listen, I don't know about you fellas—"

"Fellas?" Ringo interrupted. "I'll have you know—"

"Ringo," the driver called over his shoulder.

"But he said I was a fella, and it's clear I'm not."

Paul scoffed. "It is?"

"Don't you start!" Ringo hollered. "I'll come over there and—"

"Enough," the driver shouted. "Both of you." He refocused on Ned. "You were saying?"

"You know how things are." Ned waved the pen over the register. "I gotta fill this out or the boss will get after me. Probably fire me."

"The boss." The driver aimed his revolver at Ned. "Let's talk about him. What's his name? Where's he live?"

"Why's that matter?"

"I'm gonna give you to the count of two."

"Not three?"

"One."

"Mister Hendershot," Ned said. "He lives in Casper."

With exaggerated motion, Ned turned to the front cover of the registration book. A name and address for Herman Hendershot were listed there. Anyone who called the number would be directed to a U.S. Marshal emergency line.

"If you want," Ned said, "you can call him."

The driver scratched the top of his beanie, which pulled the cap back slightly. It revealed silver hair underneath. His brow furrowed as he repeatedly muttered, "Hendershot."

"*Mister*," Ned said. "Mr. Hendershot. He likes to be called that." It was a lie, but Ned felt that embellishing some at that moment wouldn't hurt. "He's old school."

"How old?"

"Seventies, I guess."

"Right," the driver said. "What's he look like?"

"Old. Lots of wrinkles."

"Anything else?"

"Some gray hair."

"Old people tend to have that." The driver frowned. "That's the best you can give me? Old man Hendershot, huh?"

It seemed that the driver didn't believe the lie, which irritated Ned. The guy was committing a felony, yet he couldn't provide the common courtesy of believing a simple untruth. He frowned. "About that name for the register?"

The driver waggled the barrel of the gun. "Use one of these. You can pick."

Ned narrowed his eyes as he studied the silver-haired man. "I suppose either is fine, but I'm gonna say that you look more like a Wesson."

The gun barrel dipped as the driver's brow furrowed. "Excuse me?"

"It's your eyes," Ned said. "Definitely a Wesson."

"The heck does that mean?"

Ned bent over the register book. "Is that one S or two?"

The driver tapped his gun barrel on the counter. "Elvis."

He looked up. "Hold on, I'm writing."

"Scratch it out. They call me Elvis."

Ned straightened and crossed his arms. For a moment, he studied the man across from him. "Yeah. I don't know."

"What's not to know?" the driver said. "I'm telling you, that's what they call me."

The silver-haired man looked nothing like the anointed King of Rock & Roll. Ned also had a bad turn with a ceramic version of Elvis while in California, so he wasn't thrilled with the prospect of calling this man by that name. He bent to continue writing.

The driver stabbed the register with the gun barrel. "What're you doing?"

"You said I could pick. I don't think it's one S. It doesn't look right."

"But I just told you what it was." The driver called over his shoulder. "Tell him."

Murmurs from the others offered tepid support.

"See?" The driver cocked his head. "What'd I tell you?"

Ned set down his pen and straightened. "Elvis?"

"That's right." He motioned behind him. "And we call my friends—"

"I already figured it."

Elvis nodded with pride. "You're a fan of the greats, I see."

While Ned didn't appreciate the music of Elvis Presley, he did respect what the Beatles did for rock and roll, especially the song "Helter Skelter." Many claimed that it was the origin of heavy metal. At least Elvis hadn't been sacrilegious enough to name his crew after a truly great band like Mötley Crüe. Ned would have taken considerable offense then.

Elvis tapped the registration book with his gun. "Give us the room keys."

Ned slowly dragged his thumb across the tip of his nose. He knew how things worked. He'd been a part of an intimidation ploy while with the Dawgs. Now that he was on the other side, he didn't like it. Being a better man meant standing up to bullies, even in situations like this. He wouldn't make things easy for this group.

He hunched over the registration book. "Is Rolling Stones with one L or two?"

Elvis slapped his free hand onto the book. "It's the Beatles!"

Ned sniffed. "Oh, the Beatles. Right." He gently closed the registration book on the driver's fingers. "I'm not sure how I didn't know that."

Elvis yanked his hand out from underneath the cover. While he tucked his gun back into his belt, his gaze drifted over the signs on the counter. He flicked one with a finger. "No swearing? What's wrong with foul language? You some sort of weirdo?"

He shook his head.

"A religious freak, then?"

"My grandmother taught me better."

Ringo and Paul laughed. Elvis held up a hand to stop their chatter. His eyes went to the ceiling, and he cringed. "And what's this garbage you're listening to?" His eyes dropped back to Ned. "Turn it off."

Ned reached for the radio as the song ended, and the announcer came on.

"Hold it," Elvis said.

"*All right, all right, boys and girls! It's Headbanger Harv and Classic 106.9. We're bringing the heat on this cold and snowy night. Snuggle in and stay warm with hot molten metal!"* His voice dropped an octave. *"Back to our breaking news story."*

Ned's fingers hovered over the stereo's power button.

"State and local police have called off the manhunt for the suspects involved in the robbery of the National Bank of Wyoming due to the severity of the regional blizzard. Officials are now estimating that half a million dollars was stolen. The suspects were last seen fleeing in a white Chevy van."

Ned glanced over his shoulder to Elvis. Both men then looked to the white van parked in front of the store.

"At this time, little is known except five men were involved. Law enforcement expects them to still be traveling together."

"Men," Ringo said. "What is with these people and their word choices? Don't they know that's how the patriarchy controls us?"

Elvis waved for her to stop talking.

"With highways closed in Sweetwater, Carbon, and Natrona counties, the suspects aren't expected to get far. Anyone with information about their whereabouts is encouraged to contact the authorities." Harv's voice returned to normal. *"Phew. They sure made that sound terrifying! I think they did that so everyone would stay off the roads in the snowstorm. And now this timeless beauty from White Lion."*

Elvis dragged his hand across his throat. "Turn it off."

Ned pressed a button, and the store fell silent. When he turned around, Elvis studied him.

"Is this going to be a problem?"

"Not for me. I don't like White Lion."

Elvis rubbed a hand over his mouth. "Ringo was right. There's something off about you."

"I told you," she said. "Didn't I tell you? I could sense it the moment I saw him."

Elvis held up a hand for her to stop talking.

"Right," she said. "I get it. I'll stop talking now, but you never give my intuition enough credit. I figured by now you would appreciate what I bring to the group—"

"Ringo," Elvis called out.

The woman's boots squeaked on the floor as she hurried over. "You want me to find out the truth about him?"

"No. I—"

"I'd be happy to." She eyed Ned and flexed her arms. "I'm not scared of him."

"The phone lines," Elvis said.

Ringo eyed the leader. "What about them?"

"Go outside and cut them."

"But it's cold out there." She studied the phone on the counter. "Couldn't we just unplug it in here? Or cut the line if you want." She made her fingers into a pair of scissors and mimed cutting twice. "Snip, snip."

Elvis stared at her.

"I'm just saying," Ringo said.

"Go outside—"

"Is this because I keep talking? Because I'll stop. I promise." She dragged her fingers across her lips. "I'll zip it. Just like that. Let me unplug the phone, and then I'll zip my lips, and no more words'll come out."

Elvis bared his teeth. "Go outside."

"Because if you look at that snow," Ringo said, "it's coming down something crazy and I wasn't built to be out in it." She chuckled. "Who was? Am I right?"

Elvis cocked his head. "Make sure the bungalow lines are cut, too."

"Fine," Ringo said. "But if I freeze to death out there, you'll regret it." She brushed past Paul and shoved open the door.

The bell warbled upon her exit.

Elvis curled his lip. "George."

The big man stepped away from the cooler. "Yeah?"

"Don't sound so thrilled. Kill that—" Elvis glanced at the no swearing sign. "—doorbell."

George considered the bell for a moment, then looked around. He grabbed the mop from the bucket and slopped it onto the floor. Water went everywhere.

Ned pointed at the slick linoleum. "That's a safety hazard."

The boring man shrugged. "Hey, I'm sorry, but I've gotta do this."

"You're sorry?" Elvis asked.

"I was being polite."

"Be polite on your own time." Elvis pointed at the bell. "Deal with that."

George held the handle at an angle.

"The floor won't dry very quick," Ned said. "Somebody could slip and fall."

"Give it a rest," Elvis said.

"You're not the one who's going to get sued. If your guy falls down—"

"He won't."

George stomped the handle, and it snapped near the mop head.

Ned lifted his hands in embellished frustration. "That's fantastic. Now, I'll never get the water up."

"Let it go," Elvis said. "It's not your business."

"But who's going to clean it up? Not me. You?" Ned really hammed it up. He was never in a school play as a kid, but right now, he had the feeling he might have been great at it.

George carried the broken handle over to the door. He shoved upward with the rounded end. It bounced several times before the bell popped away from the door frame.

"Is that really necessary?" Ned asked.

"I'm warning you," Elvis said.

Paul stepped forward. "Let me warn him."

"Easy," Elvis said.

George reached up and yanked on the doorbell until it came free from its wiring. He tossed the little hunk of plastic to Elvis, then pushed the door open. No entry noise was made.

"Much better," Elvis said. He eyed Ned. "No comment?"

"I'm sure Mr. Hendershot will have one."

George dropped the broken handle over near

the mop bucket. The jagged edge landed on top of the mop head. "Tell Mr. Hendershot I'm sorry."

Ned frowned. "I'm sure that'll go a long way with him."

Elvis looked outside as the heavy snowfall continued. The bright light from the pylon sign was still visible, but reading its text was impossible. "Turn off the vacancy sign," Elvis said.

Ned walked to the back of the store and flicked off a breaker. The lower portion of the pylon signed darkened. When he returned to the front, Elvis tossed the broken doorbell on the counter.

"What's your name?" Elvis asked.

"Ned."

"That's your real name?"

The question surprised Ned, but he did his best to hide it. "You think I'd pick that?"

"Someone did."

"My mother, but if you're letting me pick a new one, I want to be Nikki."

Elvis frowned. "Why?"

"Nikki Sixx from Mötley Crüe— No, wait. I want to be Lemmy from Motörhead."

"Never mind," Elvis said.

"Wait. Scratch that. I want to be Ozzy." He flashed double devil's horns. "The Prince of Darkness." Ned was now thoroughly convinced he could have been the lead in a school play.

"Hold on," Paul said. "If he gets to pick his nickname, then I want a new one."

"No," Elvis said.

Paul flicked his hand. "But his name is going to be cooler than ours. I want to be The Undertaker."

Elvis rolled his eyes. Without looking back, he said, "No one is changing their names. Understood?"

Ned shrugged. "That's fine with me. I like my name." He didn't really like this one, but it was better than Skeeter, the name Marshal Goodspeed had assigned him while in Chicago.

"We're not here to hurt you," Elvis said.

"You got a funny way of showing it."

"We're not screwing around." He pointed at the registration book. "Are we done?"

Ned slid it to the side. He reached for the pegboard and pulled down the keys for bungalows three and four. After he handed them to Elvis, the other man considered them for a moment.

"How many bungalows you got?"

Ned didn't lie. There was no reason to attempt such a thing. All the man had to do was go around back, and he'd see how many there were. "Five," he said.

Elvis studied the pegboard. Only the keys for the fifth unit remained. "Who's in the first?"

"I am."

"You live on-site?" Elvis rolled down his lip. "All by yourself?"

Ned nodded once. "Part of my compensation."

"Who's in two?" When Ned didn't respond quickly enough, Elvis grabbed the registration book, spun it around, and flipped it open. "You've got some guests."

"They're waiting out the storm like you."

"Not like us," Elvis said. He pushed the registration book away. "John."

The tall man reluctantly stepped forward.

"Some civilians are in bungalow two. Pay them a visit and make sure they understand our situation."

"Yeah, okay."

"Make sure you destroy their cell phones."

John raised his hand in acknowledgment and ambled for the door. As he exited, Ringo grabbed the door and stepped inside. Snow covered her head and shoulders.

"The phone lines are down." She blew into her hands and rubbed them together. "Took a lot more than I thought. You know it's not as easy as people want to believe."

"Ringo."

"I mean, you've got to make sure—"

"Ringo!"

"What?"

"Did you cut the phone lines for the bungalows?"

She frowned. "You mean I gotta stay out in the cold?"

Elvis tossed her a key. "After that, get warm in the third unit. We'll bring the van around."

"Fine, but I think you're doing this to punish me."

"Do you want me to send a man in your place?"

She stopped blowing in her hands, and her eyes narrowed. "I see what you did there."

"Well?"

"I'll do it." Ringo yanked the door open. "But it's under protest." She stepped back into the night.

Elvis considered his remaining men before returning his attention to Ned. "You're taking all of this well."

"Thank you."

"It wasn't meant to be a compliment." Elvis rubbed his chin. "What was it? Did you see some combat in the Coast Guard or something?"

"I have a cat."

Elvis frowned. "Huh?"

"They're calming." He mimed petting a cat even though he'd only done it once. Okay, maybe twice. "It's good for the soul or something."

Elvis glanced back at Paul, who shrugged in response.

Ned continued. "Although Travis—that's the cat—he's usually a menace, knocking stuff off counters and shelves. I think this cold weather has him off his game."

Elvis crossed his arms. "Is this how you usually are?"

"Hard to tell. I don't usually get robbed."

"Well, act normal," Elvis said. "How late does the business stay open?"

"Until eleven."

Elvis checked his watch. "Four hours." He

grunted. "We don't want any looky-loos creating situations, understand? If anyone shows up during that time, sell them what they need, then run them off."

"Why don't you just have him shut down now?" Paul asked.

"Because," Elvis said, "everything has to look normal."

"There's a blizzard out there. Shutting down would be normal."

Elvis cocked his head. "Are you questioning me?"

"At least have him turn off the rest of the sign. It don't make sense."

"We need it on—for a little while longer. Trust me." Elvis looked at Ned, and his brow furrowed. He yanked out his gun and pointed it at him. "And you. Show a little fear, would ya? Make us all feel better."

It wasn't the first time Ned had been in a situation with violent men, and it wasn't the first time a gun was pointed at him. He lifted his hands and dully said, "Yipes."

Elvis let the gun barrel droop. "This is why I don't trust you." He stuck his tongue under his lower lip. His eyes narrowed, and Ned could see a new level of distrust building. "Paul will stay here with you."

The man near the window scowled at Ned. "Me and you, princess."

Ned didn't like any of the crew who had entered his store, but he found he disliked Paul the most.

"You watch this guy," Elvis said, "like our lives depend on it. Got it, Paul?"

The chubby man nodded.

"At eleven, you close the business like normal. Then Paul and you will go back to your bungalow. In the morning, we'll be gone. Until then, we're gonna wait out the storm like everyone else. Got a bag?"

Ned reached down and pulled out a brown sack. He set it on the counter.

"George," Elvis said. "Fill it with rations."

The boring man grabbed the bag and moved about the store. He tossed food into it. He stopped at a cooler door and called over his shoulder. "Are microwaves in the rooms?"

Ned nodded.

"Yes," Elvis said.

George yanked open the door and swooped his arm over several shelves filled with frozen burritos and Hot Pockets. When the bag was full, George moved near his boss. "Ready."

Elvis said, "Put your hands on the counter."

He did as he was told.

"Paul, check behind the counter." The other man moved. "Ned, if you take your hands off the counter—"

"I won't."

Elvis and Ned stared at each other while Paul rifled through the drawers and under-the-shelf contents. When satisfied, Paul looked up and said, "Clear." He walked out from behind the counter and resumed his position in the middle of the store.

"Relax, Ned," Elvis said. "The hard part is done."

Ned stuck his hands in his pockets.

"Now," Elvis said, "Business as usual. Understand?"

"Yeah."

Elvis stepped back, spun on his heel, then headed toward the door. George was a couple of steps behind him.

When the door shut, Paul faced Ned. "Just so you know, if you do something stupid, I'm happy to lock this place up and go to bed."

Ned didn't need help understanding the threat.

Chapter 8

Several minutes passed before Paul sat on a stack of beer cases. He put his elbows on his knees and keenly watched Ned.

Ned studied his own reflection in the window. While he did so, he worked on a plan.

The first thing he needed was a weapon. He wondered how many guns Paul carried. Was it two like Elvis? It wouldn't matter if he got close enough. Ned had disarmed men with guns before, and he wasn't scared to do such a thing again. Guns in the mix made things more challenging, but that wouldn't stop events from happening.

Ned's thoughts returned to his desire to be a better man. He wouldn't want to kill Paul while disarming him. The prior version of himself wouldn't have been concerned with such matters. That version would have taken swift, violent action and ended things.

Why did being better feel harder? Was it because it was still new and unfamiliar? Did being good come naturally to people like Marshals Goodspeed and Onderdonk? Or did they question their actions like Ned, too?

Paul sucked something through his teeth and turned to look out the windows. Even saying nothing, the man irritated Ned. Did wanting to punch Paul make him a bad man? He hoped not because he was having trouble quieting those thoughts.

Ned had to act soon. Otherwise, a decision would be made for him. Elvis and his band of misfit Beatles forced this situation upon him. Either he could play it meekly, or he could fight back. The feeling deep in his gut told him what he should do right now.

He straightened.

"Where you from?" Paul asked.

Ned paused. The question's purpose seemed twofold—to interrupt thoughts of escape and to get him to lower his defenses. Paul must have guarded someone before.

"Hermiston." It was part of the Ned Delahanty background that Goodspeed insisted he learn.

"Never heard of it."

"It's in Oregon."

"Is it nice?"

Ned had no idea, so he shrugged. If forced to, he'd lie about it being a nice place. He believed most folks did that about the city where they grew up. It might have been a horrible town, yet they'd tell a stranger it was nice, maybe a little small or confining, but still generally a good place to raise a family. However, they fled the town for somewhere more exciting.

Right now, Ned didn't want to blather on about a place he'd never lived. A plan was starting to formulate—he only had to get close enough to Paul to execute it. He moved toward the end of the counter.

Paul stiffened. "Where do you think you're

going?"

"To stock the shelves."

The man slipped off the beer cases and stuck his hand on the gun in his waistband. "You stay over there, princess. Don't come any closer."

"I usually stock the shelves at this time of night."

"This ain't a usual night, or did you forget?" He motioned in the direction of the counter. "Stay over there, and we'll get along fine. Got it?"

Ned returned to his spot near the cash register. The only noise in the shop was the hum of the overhead lights. He needed a new plan. "Mind if we listen to the radio?" Even cruddy eighties rock was better than silence.

"I don't care." Paul released the gun handle and returned to his sitting position on the beer cases. "Turn it to a country station."

Ned grunted. "Never mind."

"What's with you? Turn on the radio and find a country station."

This wasn't an argument worth having. Ned reached for the radio just as a pair of headlights pierced the darkness and veil of falling snow. A silver Lincoln Navigator bounced through the parking lot and proceeded toward the building. It slid to a stop in front of the Quik N Go.

As the family of six gathered outside the store, Paul stood. "Act cool."

Ned chuckled. "Oh, don't worry about me." He flicked on the radio, and a guitar screeched through the flimsy speakers.

"Hey," Paul hissed. "Turn that garbage off."

The family tumbled into the store. When the four girls heard the music, they squealed with laughter.

"Yeah!" the youngest yelled. She spread her arms out and spun them like two buzz saws. She raced down an aisle.

The oldest child shook her head. "That's not how you do it." She proceeded to windmill sideways down a separate aisle.

The other two girls scattered in opposite directions, twirling as they went. Chattering laughter drowned out the music.

"Girls!" Hattie called. She stomped her feet on the entry mat and looked apologetically at Paul. "They've been cooped up."

Paul stared at her with a flat, uninterested look.

Hattie's eyes briefly widened then she glanced at her husband, who only offered a shrug of support. She hurried after her children. "Girls! Girls! Stop this instant. There are others here."

Alden stamped his feet a couple of times. "How you doing?" he said to Paul but didn't bother to wait for the man's reply. He faced Ned. "You believe this snow?" He brushed the powder from his shoulders. "It's murder out there."

"About to be in here, too," Paul said. "Turn off that music."

"No!" the children screamed in unison. They chanted, "Rock, rock, rock," as they jumped in front of the spinner rack filled with hats. Hattie stood nearby.

Ned asked, "Did they eat their candy?"

Alden stepped toward the counter. "Right after we left. Hey, tell me you got a bungalow left. I saw the vacancy sign was turned off, but everything else was lit up, so I figured we had to take a chance. Worst you could tell us is no."

Paul exaggeratedly shook his head. "This is what I was talking about. We should have turned everything off."

"What's that?" Alden asked.

Ned cleared his throat. "There's one bungalow left."

"Yes!" Alden's face broadened with a smile. "You are a lifesaver, my friend."

One of the girls screamed, "Lifesavers!" The others shrieked, "Yeah!"

"Girls," Hattie hollered. "No shouting!"

"How many beds are there?" Alden asked.

"Two."

"It'll be a tight fit, but we'll take it." Alden shook his head. "Roads are a mess. Nearly impassable. Most folks are gonna be stuck up on the mountain for the night. I feel sorry for them." He glanced over his shoulder at Paul. "You working the late shift?"

"No."

The four girls waved at Paul as they skipped passed him.

Hattie admonished them. "Girls, stop that and come back here this minute."

They spun in circles, bumping into each other as they arrived back at the hat spinner.

Paul pulled a small walkie-talkie from an inner pocket of his coat. He stepped into the cooler.

Alden returned his attention to Ned. "Not much of a conversationalist, your friend."

Ned leaned in. "You should go. Leave now."

"Go?" Alden's face scrunched in disbelief. "Are you nuts?"

"That man is—"

Alden pointed at the window. "The roads out there are an ice rink. We barely made it here. There's no way we're leaving. I'm taking that room. I don't care how grumpy your friend is."

Ned shrugged. "Have it your way." He set the register book on the counter.

"Hats, hats, hats!" the girls chanted. They jumped up and down in front of the spinner.

"Driver's license," Ned said.

"Man, my luck is finally changing." Alden smiled, then lowered his voice. "I had to come on this ski trip, you know, but then this snowstorm happened which was great all in itself, but now we've lucked out with this room." He glanced over his shoulder before continuing. "Tell me the room is bad. I mean, it's a gas station bungalow, so it's gotta be bad, right?"

Ned shrugged a single shoulder. "It's not great."

"Oh, this is sweet." Alden excitedly handed Ned his driver's license. "Things are finally breaking my way."

The card read that Alden Fodey was from Overland Park, Kansas.

"Put those back," Hattie said.

"But dad said we could," the oldest child

protested.

Each of the girls had put on a hat then. The youngest wore an orange beanie, while the three oldest girls wore blue trucker hats. The caps had oddly suggestive logos like *Make it Quik N Go* and *I Got Some at Quik N Go,* and *Quik N Go Gave Me Gas.* No one had purchased a single hat since Ned started there.

Alden rested his elbows on the counter. "Maybe we'll get snowed in for days. How great would that be?" He chuckled to himself. "Diabolical."

Ned lifted an eyebrow.

"She'll never want to go skiing again. That's how she is." He tapped his temple. "Gotta think ahead in situations like this. Marriage is a game of attrition—who can outlast the other. She's taken a lot of ground in the last couple years." He looked over his shoulder at his bouncing daughters. "Brought in some reinforcements."

Overhead, the song ended, and an announcer came on. "*Wow-whee folks, that was the Vinnie Vincent Invasion with 'Boyz are Gonna Rock.' That's like an eighties' love song.*" Harv sighed. "*Anyway, this is Headbanger Harv and Classic 106.9 keeping you toasty warm through the night!*"

"You might want to listen to this," Ned said. His eyes went toward the ceiling.

Alden waved him off. "This is my dad's music."

"I'm talking the news."

"Ugh. Even worse."

The announcer's voice changed to a gravelly serious tone. *"Following up on our breaking news story, state and Casper authorities are—"*

The cooler door banged open, and Paul stepped out. "Turn it off."

Alden glanced over his shoulder.

"Mind your own business," Paul said, "if you know what's good for you."

The father's eyes widened. He whispered to Ned, "What's up with your friend?"

"Rough day."

The oldest girl squealed in delight as she slid through the puddled water on the floor. The next one followed right behind her. The smallest fell on her bottom. She scrambled to her feet and followed her sisters back through the water again.

"Girls," Hattie said. It seemed that she was trying to stop their game or, at least, quiet them. Perhaps she simply patted the air in a desperate act of pushing their noise away. "Put those hats back."

"Dad promised!" they cried in unison.

Ned flicked off the radio.

Alden snickered. "Rough day whatever. Your friend should try living with four little girls. That would toughen him up."

"What's that?" Paul said. He stepped over to the counter. "Who needs toughening up?"

Alden tried to affect an innocent look, but it succeeded in only making him look more guilty. "We were talking about—" His eyes flashed around the counter, and he grabbed a beef jerky stick from a nearby box. "—how tough this stuff is."

Paul opened his coat and revealed the gun in his belt.

Alden's eyes widened. "Are we getting robbed?" He grinned. "Oh, man, this is fantastic. I mean it. A blizzard, a gas station bungalow, *and* a robbery. It's like a vacation trifecta."

"I'm not kidding around," Paul said. "Put your phone on the counter and shut up."

Alden's gaze locked on to the revolver. "Wait a minute. You're not robbing the joint?"

"Better do it," Ned said.

Paul rested his hand on the butt of the weapon. "Listen to the man."

"What did I do?" Alden jiggled the beef jerky.

"You picked the wrong convenience store."

Alden slipped the jerky back into its box. "We can go somewhere else. In fact, we'll leave right now." He called over his shoulder. "Wrap it up, ladies. We're leaving."

"We want a hat!" the youngest girl cried.

"Too late." Paul kept his hand on his gun and waggled his elbow. "Your phone on the counter—now."

Alden reached into his jacket, slowly pulled out his cell phone, and set it down.

"Now your wife's," Paul said.

"I don't carry her phone."

Paul leaned forward. Through gritted teeth, he said, "Then go get it."

Alden nervously laughed. "Right." From the

side of his mouth, he called, "Hattie."

"What?"

"Bring your phone over here."

"Can't you see what I'm dealing with?"

The children squealed once more. They seemed overjoyed that their mother was attempting to stop their mischief. One of them hid behind a beer display. Another darted in between the aisles. The third spun in circles. And the fourth ran down the hallway to the closed restroom.

"Hattie," Alden forcefully said, "I need your phone."

She stopped and looked his way. "Why? Aren't you getting service?"

He fully faced her now. "*Please.*" He clasped his hands together. "For the love of everything holy."

Hattie pulled her phone from a pocket. As she walked over, she activated its screen. "I'm not getting any service, either. I thought this new provider was supposed to be—"

Paul released his grip on his gun and let his coat fall closed.

Alden snapped his fingers and held out his hand.

Hattie's lips pursed. "Don't you act that way with me, Alden Fodey."

"Give it to me," he said softly. "Please."

She eyed the other men, then reluctantly handed her husband the phone. Alden placed it on the counter next to his.

"What's going on?" she asked.

"I'll tell you in a minute." Alden eyed Paul. "Now, go back with the kids."

"Stop telling me what to do, Alden. I'm not your property. Just because I bore your children doesn't mean you get to talk to me that way."

Paul yanked open his coat like a flasher in a supermarket. Hattie jumped back in shock. When she realized what she was looking at, her eyes widened further. She looked to her husband, then to Ned, then back to her husband. She was about to ask a question, but her gaze flicked to the gun again. "I'll go back with the girls."

"Stay right here," Paul said. He closed his coat. "We're about to get this thing sorted out." To Ned, he said, "What bungalow are you putting them in?"

"Five." Ned retrieved a key from the board and handed it to Alden.

Ringo arrived at the front door and stepped in. She was about to say something when the children screamed as they passed by. Their arms windmilled as they spun in circles. Now all of them wore blue Quik N Go baseball caps. Ringo's lip curled, and she muttered, "Kids."

Ned pointed at the *No Swearing* sign, but no one caught his motion.

Ringo moved closer to her associate. "What's the plan?"

Paul motioned toward Alden. "Dad walks with you. Mom drives the fancy rig around back." He eyed Hattie. "Can you do that?"

She nodded. "Of course, I know how to drive."

"Try anything stupid, and Ringo will dust your old man."

"Dust?"

Ringo dragged a finger across her throat.

"Nothing stupid." Hattie's face blanched. "Got it."

Paul eyed Ringo. "Where's Elvis?"

"Working on a new plan."

"Good," Paul said. "That's good. We just need to give him some time. He'll get us out of here."

Chapter 9

When the store was quiet again, Paul studied Ned. "I don't trust you," he said.

"There's a lot of that going around."

"Why don't you scare?"

"I scare plenty," Ned said.

That wasn't a lie. The things that put fear into Ned were things he couldn't control. The power of the government scared him. When they came after him while he was with the Dawgs, there wasn't anything he could do but wait for their metaphorical anvil to drop on top of his head. He couldn't fight back.

But Ned wasn't scared now. These men could be seen. They could be touched. Ned figured he'd fight back soon enough. Therefore, fear never entered the equation—only caution.

Paul moved forward. "So, you're scared now?"

"Sure," Ned lied.

"You don't look it."

"I hide it. Deep down."

Paul grunted. "I don't like it when people aren't scared. It makes me... uncomfortable." He tapped his stomach. "In here."

Ned pointed toward a shelf. "Antacids are on the bottom."

"Mr. Smart Mouth." Paul frowned. "Are you always this helpful?"

"Customer service is its own reward."

A pair of headlights pierced the darkness and the gusting snow.

"Act cool," Paul said.

"Like before."

Paul cast a sideways glance. "See? That's what I'm saying. That kind of stuff bothers me. Show some concern for your safety and get rid of these jokers."

The Land Rover Defender proceeded through the parking lot. When it slid to a stop at the front of the building, the lights clicked off, and the engine silenced. Donovan climbed out of the passenger seat. His passenger joined him this time. They both hurried to the front of the store. Once inside, they stomped their feet on the mat.

Donovan pulled the knitted cap with the fuzzy ball from his head. He slapped it against his leg. The woman left her cap on. She wore a beige snow suit and dark brown snow boots.

"I see you shoveled the walkway," Donovan said, "but it can probably use it again."

"Let it be." The woman rolled her eyes.

He put his hands on his hips and considered her. "I'm only being helpful."

"We're a little busy," Ned said.

Donovan faced him. "Busy?" His brow furrowed as he briefly considered Paul. When his attention returned to Ned, he said, "There's only us here."

"Lots of stuff going on."

"Sophia and I barely made it back." Donovan pointed outside. "The roads are atrocious. Nearly a disaster."

Hearing her name, the woman smiled apologetically. "He's being dramatic."

Donovan's gaze snapped to her. "Dramatic?"

"It's only a little snow," she said.

"That's a blizzard, Sophia. The state closed the roads. They don't do that for a little snow."

She rolled her eyes again. "Oh, relax, Donny. Do you want me to drive?"

Donovan extended his hands. "We never even made the mountain, which they also closed."

Sophia stared at him.

"I thought we were going to die."

"*Puh*-lease."

"You thought we were going to die, too."

She looked to Paul, then Ned, and shook her head. "No, I didn't."

"Yes, you did. What's up with you? Why are you being this way?"

"Stop crying." She motioned Donovan toward the counter. "Ask him."

Donovan frowned, then turned to Ned. "Got a bungalow available?"

"They're all rented."

He threw his hands up in frustration. "Great. Just great. Now, what do we do?"

"Oh, stop," Sophia said. She moved toward Ned. "We're gonna park in your lot for the night. Is that okay?"

"Fine with me."

The idea of folks from the mountain resting in the parking lot hadn't occurred to him before then. But if the lot filled up with vehicles, Elvis and his men couldn't do anything to him or the others. They'd be forced to leave. Ned liked the idea and wondered how he could encourage others to do such a thing. Maybe he should go out to the pylon sign and change the lettering to invite travelers to park for the night.

"Put them in your bungalow," Paul said.

Ned eyed him.

Donovan's face brightened. "What's that?"

"He heard me," Paul said. He tugged the walkie-talkie from his pocket and keyed it. "Elvis, this is Paul. We got a situation."

The radio squelched, and Elvis answered. "*I'll send George.*"

Donovan and Sophia exchanged glances.

"What's going on?" she asked.

"The good Samaritan over there," Paul said, "is gonna give you his room." He eyed Ned. "Isn't that right, princess?"

"If you say so." Ned dug into his pocket, pulled out a set of keys, and tossed them onto the counter. "The door sticks, so give it a shove. Be warned. There's a cat."

"We can't take your keys," Sophia said.

Paul opened his coat and revealed the gun in his waistband. "Take them."

Donovan hurriedly grabbed the keys from the counter.

"What's going on here?" Sophia asked.

Ned cocked his head. "Haven't you listened to the radio?"

Donovan and Sophia said simultaneously, "We stream."

Paul raised a single eyebrow. "So you've

missed the news?"

"We never pay attention to it." Sophia waved her hand. "It's all fake."

"A shame, too," Paul said. "You can't believe anything you hear anymore."

George hurried by the front window. Snow covered his head and shoulders. He stepped inside and considered the two customers. "What are we doing?" he asked.

Paul moved toward him. "Put them in bungalow one." He lifted his chin toward Ned. "His place."

George's shoulders slumped. "We keep digging a deeper hole."

"Enough with that talk." Paul turned to Donovan and Sophia. "Pull out your phones."

Donovan quickly produced his, but Sophia said, "I don't have one."

Paul's eyes narrowed. "If I search you and find one, we're going to have a problem."

She jammed her hand into a pocket and came out with a cell phone.

"Get those, George, and throw them into the snow."

George grabbed both cell phones. He walked outside and hurtled them in opposite directions.

"Well, that's just great," Donovan said. "We don't have the insurance on those."

Paul chuckled. "That's the least of your worries."

George leaned into his associate's ear and whispered something. A couple of seconds later, the two separated.

Paul said, "All right, pretty boy, you walk with George here. And the lady will bring around the car. Make sure you keep an eye on her, George."

Donovan and Sophia shuffled forward a couple of steps.

"If either of you tries anything stupid—" Paul dragged a finger across his throat. "Got it?"

The couple nodded.

"Then get going."

When the three left the store, Paul said, "Turn off the lights. All of them, including those on the highway."

"I thought your boss wanted us to look like we were open."

"He did, but I'm making a command decision."

Ned pointed to a spot at the rear of the store. "The panel's back there."

Paul pulled the gun from his waistband. "I know, and I'm not stopping you. Turn them off."

Ned took his time getting to the switches. Outside, the pylon sign darkened, as did the gas pump canopy. The building's exterior lights flicked off then the interior lights. Only a single emergency light remained on.

"We should have shut you down right away," Paul said. "Saved ourselves this hassle with the additional customers."

"Why didn't you?"

"Elvis makes the rules."

"Why's that?"

Paul sneered. "Stop talking. You keep making

me more suspicious."

Ned stood in the middle of the store and looked around. "What are we going to do now?"

"You and me are going to sit here in the dark and do nothing while Elvis is back there in his bungalow living his best life."

"The bungalows aren't that nice," Ned said.

"Better than up here with you. Get back behind the counter."

Ned returned to his position near the register. He rested his elbows on the counter. He better finalize a plan soon because he had a pretty good idea of what was about to happen.

Sooner or later, Elvis was going to realize that no one should be left alive come morning.

***

Ned finally had a plan.

It wasn't a great one, he readily admitted. It was born more from desperation than careful consideration. He would bound over the counter, land on his feet, and attack Paul.

There were a few assumptions in that plan. First, that he could actually vault over the counter. It was waist height, and he'd start from a standing position. As clandestinely as he could, he cleared the counter of items that might hinder his leap. He moved the store policy signs out of the way.

Paul eyed him. "What are you doing?"

"Tidying up."

The chubby guard grunted something and

returned his attention to the falling snow.

After making sure the counter was clear, Ned squatted and then stood. He repeated this motion several times.

"You okay over there?" Paul asked.

"A little stiff. Trying to work out a kink." Ned continued with his deep knee bends.

"Well, knock it off. You're bugging me."

Ned stopped squatting. He pushed out his right heel and stretched his calf muscle. The more he considered the height and width of the counter, the less confident he became of clearing it in a single bound. He had no doubt he could get on top of it, but it would be in a messy scramble rather than a clean jump.

He stretched the other calf. His eyes went up to the cigarette holder. It hung from the ceiling and extended down to his forehead. That meant Ned would have to keep low when going over the counter. Otherwise, he'd smack his head on the hanging rack.

Paul slipped from the stack of beer. "Don't do anything stupid. I can see you thinking about something."

Ned was about to ask what the man was talking about when a pair of headlights bounced through the parking lot. A white pickup with a light bar pulled parallel with the convenience store. Its headlights shone into the distance and provided a cone of light for the snow to fall through gently. Metal snow chains were wrapped around the tires. Vinyl lettering ran the length of the truck, which read *Natrona County*

Sheriff.

"Elvis," Paul said into his walkie-talkie. "Red alert. Red alert!"

The radio crackled before Elvis answered. *"Cops?"*

Paul shook his radio while he transmitted, "Isn't that what red alert means?"

There was a long pause as Paul waited for Elvis to respond.

Finally, Paul lifted the radio to his lips. "Yes. The cops. The cops are here!"

"How many?"

"One truck."

"On my way. Keep cool. Don't do anything stupid. I repeat—"

Paul clicked off his radio and slid it into his coat. He backpedaled deeper into the store. "Say anything, and both you and the cop get it."

A deputy climbed out of the still-running vehicle. He wore a brown winter coat with an open slit over the gun on his left hip. He appeared to be in his fifties and walked with the confident gait of someone comfortable with his authority.

The deputy yanked open the door and stepped inside. His eyes drifted upward to the dangling wires from where the bell once hung. "The heck happened?"

"Jackalopes," Ned said.

"Terrible vermin." The deputy stamped his feet on the entry mat. He noticed Paul watching him. "Can I help you?"

"No, sir." Paul pointed outside. "I was only

wondering how you're making it out and about in that snow."

"Slowly and not without some moments of worry. The highways are worse than a skating rink."

Ned eyed the nametag on the lawman's coat. "Deputy Lockwood."

"Yes, sir."

Paul's eyes snapped to Ned, and he angrily shook his head.

"The truck says you're from Natrona County, but aren't we in Freemont County?"

The deputy shrugged. "I'm a little out of my jurisdiction. You might have heard about a disturbance we had in Casper earlier today."

Paul stopped shaking his head and scowled.

"No," Ned said, "I didn't hear."

"Some boys robbed a bank and fled in a white Chevy van. You see anything like that come through here?"

Ned looked at Paul, so the deputy did, too.

"Did something like that come through here?" the deputy repeated.

"No, sir," Paul said.

"Did you guys close because of the storm?"

Ned opened his mouth to speak, but Paul interrupted him.

"Yeah," Paul said. "The storm."

"What a mess. From what I heard, they locked down the mountain. They're even pulling people out of their cars and shuttling them up to the resort in snowmobiles and snowcats." The deputy's eyes narrowed, and he looked about.

"Why *are* you boys standing in the dark?"

"We just closed," Paul said.

"And what are *you* doing back there?" the deputy asked.

Paul held up a yellow bag of Funyons. "Stocking chips."

"Get out here where I can see you. You're making me nervous." The deputy faced Ned again. "Been a month or so since I've been by here. You must be new."

"Started a few weeks ago."

"What happened to the other guy?"

"Heart attack."

The deputy cocked his head. "No kidding. I liked him." He looked to Paul. "So you didn't see five men in a white Chevy van?"

Elvis appeared on the sidewalk then. He didn't glance into the store but instead walked confidently with his eyes forward. The deputy watched Elvis approach the door.

Paul stepped even closer. "You guys have no idea what these robbers look like?" he asked.

The deputy held up a hand instead of answering.

Elvis stepped into the store. In his right hand, he clutched a gun.

The deputy reached for his, but Paul stuck his revolver to the man's head. "Don't even think about it."

Deputy Lockwood slowly lifted his hands into the air. Paul yanked the lawman's gun from its holster.

"Now, isn't this something?" Elvis asked.

Paul walked over and handed the gun to his boss. "What should we do with him?"

Elvis glanced at Ned before saying, "We're gonna hold him just like the others."

"Want me to watch him?" Paul asked.

"No, I've got this one. I'll take him back to my bungalow."

"But I'd be happy to, boss."

"You stay here." Elvis glanced around, then looked outside. "Why are all the lights out?"

"They're not all out," Paul said. "We still got the emergency one on."

"You know what I mean."

"I just thought—"

Elvis craned his head. "When have I wanted you to think?"

"But people are going to keep coming." He motioned to the deputy. "Even the cop said so."

Lockwood nodded.

Elvis seemed to consider the deputy's input. "Yeah, fine. Keep the lights off, but you're staying up here with him." Elvis motioned toward Ned.

"Why's that?"

"Because we need eyes on the road. We need to know if anything is happening."

"But—"

"But nothing," Elvis snapped. "Trust me. I know what I'm doing. You'd be wise to remember that." He waved his gun at the deputy. "Now, if you'd be so kind."

Deputy Lockwood led the way out of the building. Elvis directed him into the passenger side of the truck. Elvis walked to the driver's seat and climbed in. The truck disappeared around the side of the building.

Ned wasn't in the habit of worrying about the welfare of cops. Nonetheless, he found himself hoping that Deputy Lockwood would be safe. He seemed like an all-right guy.

Chapter 10

Paul dropped heavily onto the stack of beer cases. He angrily swiped at the flimsy sign announcing the sale price and sent it drifting to the floor. "Turn on the radio." He stiffened. "And it better be country. I'm in no mood for your screwing around."

Ned didn't fight with him this time. The conversation with Elvis had obviously put Paul in a bad mood. That was good for Ned as he wanted Paul to stew on something besides him. If Ned became a problem for the man, then Paul would lose focus on his boss and start to pay attention to him again.

Ned found an oldies country station and let it play. The singer crooned about his baby wearing blue jeans. The song was so unoffensive that it offended Ned. Paul's head bobbed in time with the tune's rhythm, and his hand patted his knee.

With his babysitter distracted, Ned got back to work on his problem. The first thing he needed to determine was where each of the crew was.

Paul was ten feet away.

George took Donovan and Sophia to the first bungalow—Ned's home. The only thing of arguable importance in the small cabin was the cat.

John left earlier to watch Kiki and Brick, who were staying in bungalow two.

And Ringo was dispatched to watch over Alden and Hattie's family in bungalow five.

That left Elvis guarding Deputy Lockwood. They could be in either bungalow three or four. Ned bet on the fourth bungalow because Elvis gave Ringo the room key to the third unit earlier, and she probably still had it.

Regardless, one wild card wasn't so bad. Ned liked those odds.

Paul's head nodded as a new song started on the radio. This one had something to do with the singer's multiple ex-wives living in Texas. Paul absently patted his knee, and his brow furrowed in concentration. It was clear he was thinking about the lyrics.

Ned needed to determine a course of action now.

He'd given up on leaping over the counter. It wouldn't work. He needed a reason to get into the middle of the store so he could be closer to Paul. Once that happened, he would overpower the man and take his gun.

That latter part wasn't as simple as it sounded, though.

Ned would have to decide what to do with Paul—secure, incapacitate, or kill.

Killing was easiest. And safest. But he didn't want to kill the man. Ned would do it if he had to, but that didn't fit with his new goal in life. Killing should be a last resort, not the go-to option.

There were many ways a man could be incapacitated. Ned could break one of Paul's bones—maybe a leg. Yet, the guy could still fire his gun with a broken tibia. Paul seemed the type who could fight through some pain. And a broken arm wouldn't do. That would hurt Paul, of course, but not as much as the leg. A fractured arm would still leave Paul mobile and able to fire with the other hand. Therefore, Ned would have to break both arms to put the man out of commission.

That would require a lot of patience from Paul. Ned couldn't rightly say, "Hey, guy, hold still while I break your arms."

Maybe Ned could knock out the guy. That would require some extraordinarily up-close and personal fighting. Ned wasn't opposed to it, but what if Paul was experienced? Even though he was chubby, he might be a capable fighter. And getting knocked out was only temporary. A few seconds. A minute, at the most. Whenever Paul came out of it, the guy would likely be groggy and disoriented, but that didn't mean he wouldn't fight again.

So, maybe it *was* kill or be killed. Ned didn't like that option. Not yet, at least.

Paul slid off the beer cases and shimmied his shoulders. It appeared he was done worrying about the disagreement with Elvis. "How can you not like this music?"

"Reminds me of someone I know."

"All great music does." Paul dipped a shoulder and danced toward the beer coolers where the mop bucket and broken handle lay. "I always think of this one girl." When Paul neared the slick area of the floor, he dipped his shoulder in the opposite direction. His feet crossed over themselves. "She was really something. Real pretty thing out of Mobile."

Ned didn't know how to dance, but when Paul dropped his shoulder, he figured he should at least try. His shoulders wobbled like an airplane without its stabilization control.

When Paul shimmied toward the back of the store again, Ned joined him. Paul danced in the middle of the store while Ned clomped and swayed behind the counter. Both of their boots squeaked and squelched as they moved.

"Look at you," Paul said. "Finally finding the spirit of country music."

Ned forced an awkward smile. "Maybe it's not so bad." It was, of course. Disco country was near the bottom of his list of musical choices—slightly above classical music yet below industrial punk.

When Paul neared the wet floor again, he lowered his shoulder, whirled, and headed in the opposite direction. His feet wiggled and crossed each other while his hips gyrated like an unbalanced washing machine.

Ned remained behind the counter as he clomped back toward the register. It was too early to attempt a move toward the middle.

At the front of the store, both men dipped their shoulders, spun, and started the opposite way. Ned hated to admit it, but Paul knew how to dance, especially by himself. Ned felt like an engine with a busted piston—always one beat from the rhythm. Perhaps Marshal Goodspeed had been right, and he didn't have coordination.

"Keep at it," Paul said with some appreciation. "You'll get it."

The encouragement from the chubby man surprised Ned. The music and dancing brought him happiness that wasn't obvious in his earlier actions.

"Try this," Paul said. He slowed his promenade and kicked his right foot out. It crossed back and forth over his left.

Behind the counter, Ned kicked the floorboard. He did it on purpose and exaggerated his discomfort. He repeatedly kicked the floorboard as he shuffled and plodded toward the opening.

"What are you doing, princess? I can't hear the song anymore."

"It's a tight fit."

Paul considered Ned but didn't stop moving. "You do look sort of crammed back there." He neared the wetness on the floor and paused. "Step out here, but don't try anything stupid."

"I just want to dance."

"It's the music," Paul said with a smile. "It'll do that to you."

Ned stepped in front of the counter.

"All right. Let's do it again." Paul glided toward the window. His right foot crisscrossed over his left then he switched feet. It was an effortless slide across the store.

Ned, on the other hand, clunked and thudded his way over the linoleum. His head bounced not in time with the song but rather with the landing of each step. He tried to float over the vinyl floor, but he looked like a heavy-footed chicken.

Paul chuckled. "Who taught you to dance?"

"No one."

"It shows. Relax your shoulders. Open those hips." Paul wriggled his whole body at the window like a dog shaking off a coat of water. "Let's try it once more."

Ned simply turned around. His clomping became an out-of-time skip to keep up with Paul.

As the two men moved back toward the cooler, the song overhead wound down. Ned's chance was now or never since Paul was near the slick spot on the linoleum.

Paul beamed with pride. "I call this dance the Gator Swamp Slide."

That's when Ned jumped. He spread his arms wide like a man leaping from an airplane.

Paul's eyes widened, and he brought his hands up. He stepped back into the puddle of water and slipped. Paul landed on the floor, and his head hit the side of the mop bucket. It flipped over and sent the broken mop handle skittering away.

Ned flopped on Paul's chest. He hoped the extra force would have knocked the wind out of Paul and ended the fight.

Paul didn't reach for his gun, which Ned had

expected. Instead, he punched upward and hit Ned in the nose. Ned immediately slugged Paul in the eye. Then he hit him a second time, which ended the fight.

Ned remained sitting on Paul's chest and touched his nose. It felt tender, and his fingers came back bloody. His eyes watered as he wriggled the bridge of his nose. It didn't feel broken, and the blood would stop soon enough. That's how it was with these things. It wasn't the first bloody nose Ned had earned.

The announcer came on. *"How about that gem, folks? This is Winny on Classy 92.9, and I'm spinning my way into your hearts on this beautiful wintery night."* She rustled a piece of paper.

Ned pulled the gun from Paul's waistband and the walkie-talkie from his coat pocket.

"We got us an update on that breaking news story." Winny crunched the paper again. *"The smokeys announced that those bad boys left the state. Supposedly, they're in Nebraska now."* Winny giggled. *"Those yellow bellies musta known the long arm of the law was getting close and slipped out under the cover of darkness."*

Ned searched Paul's pants pockets but didn't find anything—not even a wallet.

"Well, I say good riddance," Winny said, *"and let's not worry about them anymore. Instead, let's talk about the 'Harper Valley PTA.'"*

A new song started.

Ned set the gun and walkie-talkie near the cash register. He grabbed a roll of duct tape from underneath the counter and returned to Paul. It took some effort to flip the unconscious man over. The chubby man's back was wet now. Ned spun the tape around Paul's wrists. It wasn't the best tie-up job he'd ever done, but he needed it to be quick rather than permanent. Next, he tied it around Paul's ankles. When Ned finished that, he put a swath of tape over the man's mouth.

He tossed the roll of duct tape onto the counter before dragging Paul toward the restroom. Ned dug a key from his pocket and unlocked the door. He put Paul inside and stepped back to consider how secure the man was.

Even if Paul's hands and feet remained tied, the guy could stand up and open the door.

Ned ran back to the counter and collected the duct tape. When he returned to the restroom, he grabbed Paul's feet and hoisted them up. He dragged the man to the safety bar secured to the wall three feet above the floor. Ned applied a generous amount of tape to tie Paul's legs to the wall. He wasn't going anywhere now.

Paul's eyes fluttered open. He seemed confused as his gaze drifted about the restroom. When he realized his predicament, he wriggled his ankles and flopped about, but he didn't get free. After a moment of futility, he stopped fighting and glared at Ned.

"Don't do anything stupid," Ned said.

The tape muffled Paul's complaint.

Ned stepped out of the restroom and locked

it. He returned to the counter to inspect the gun. It was a Smith & Wesson revolver like the gun that Elvis brandished earlier. Ned opened it and confirmed it held six rounds.

To Ned, the revolvers seemed a strange weapon to use during a bank robbery. He would have preferred an automatic weapon like a Glock. A single Glock could carry more rounds than two revolvers.

So was everyone in the crew armed like Paul with a single gun? Or were some of the others armed like Elvis with a revolver *and* an automatic?

Ned put the gun in his pocket but immediately pulled it out. He didn't want to rely on it because he knew how easy it was for him to make it a first-choice option. Ned hid the weapon under the counter. He thought about putting it in the floor safe, but if he did need to access it quickly, he would have created a problem for himself.

He slipped on his coat and shoved the duct tape into his pocket. He put the walkie-talkie into the other and headed for the door.

Ned Delahanty stepped outside. He didn't bother locking the door before stepping into the cold night.

Chapter 11

Ned hurried along the sidewalk to the edge of the Quik N Go. He peered around the corner. Not seeing anything, he stepped as quietly as he could into the roadway and its ankle-deep snow. He knew how to be stealthy in warm weather, but acting like a ninja in the cold made no sense. He stood out among the white background, and each footfall into the powder made him feel like a clomping horse.

At this moment, Ned had choices. He could climb into his truck and make a run for it. With its snowblade down, the four-wheel drive pickup might give him a good chance of getting away. Although, if Elvis and his misfit Beatles decided to pursue him, all Ned would do is make it easy for them. But why would they pursue him? They didn't care about Ned.

Maybe the truck was still an option. Perhaps he should offer to clear the roadway for the crew. He could plow it all the way to Evanston or as far west as the storm went.

But he'd just assaulted Paul and tied the man up. It was unlikely that Elvis would forgive him for that. Paul certainly would not. Besides, would Ned want to help this crew? That would not be something a better man would do. It wouldn't be the actions of someone he'd like to see in the mirror. Was it something he'd proudly tell Daphne Winterbourne about?

Yet he was willing not to alert the police when they arrived so he could avoid being a rat. That inaction now put him in this predicament.

There seemed to be a fine line between *feeling* good and *being* good.

Ned knew he had to set things right. He hunched his shoulders and plodded through the snow toward his truck. He leaned against it and listened. Slowly, Ned peered around the edge of the vehicle to his bungalow. Donovan and Sophia should be inside with George. The lights were on, but Ned didn't see any movement. Parked next to his truck was the Land Rover.

He looked further down the road. It was too hard to see the other bungalows through the snowstorm.

Ned snuck toward the front of the nearest structure and attempted to peer through the closest window. Curtains were pulled. He moved to another window but discovered the same thing—more curtains. Not even a crack to peer through.

The radio in Ned's pocket crackled.

"Hey, Paul," Elvis called. *"Status check."*

Ned hurriedly backed away from the bungalow as he frantically pulled the radio from his coat. He almost dropped it, and the walkie-talkie bounced from hand to hand before he finally caught it.

"Paul, status check," Elvis said. *"What are you doing?"*

Ned slumped against the truck, lifted the radio to his lips, and pressed the transmit button. "Bzzzt." It was the best impression of static he could muster.

"*Say again?*"

"Bzzzt grrkl."

"*Your radio isn't transmitting correctly.*"

Ned covered his mouth with a hand. "Bzzzt grrkl dnch."

"*Replace your batteries. What about you, George? Status check.*"

The radio crackled. "*Uh, George here. All good. Nothing to worry about.*"

"Now, I'm worried."

Ned looked around his pickup to the first bungalow. A trail of footsteps led from the truck to the bungalow and back again.

"*We're all good,*" George said. "*Everything is fine, I promise.*"

"*You promise? What's wrong with you, George? Do I need to go over there?*"

"*No, no. Everything is under control.*"

There was a long pause. Ned cocked his head and waited for the door of bungalow four to burst open. He expected Elvis to stalk through the storm, fling open the door to the first bungalow, and scold George for whatever he was doing.

But that didn't happen. Instead, Elvis calmly said, "*Ringo, status check.*"

Ned patiently waited as Elvis finished the checks with Ringo and John. He then snapped off his walkie-talkie and started counting. First, he went to a hundred, but that felt too quick. So he decided to add another hundred. He knew he couldn't hear Elvis leaving his cabin, but he thought he *might* hear something. After several minutes, when he didn't see or hear anything, Ned straightened and marched toward the first bungalow.

He twisted the knob, but it was locked. Ned knocked on the door. He wanted to bang on it the way the cops did whenever they thought they were in the right. He figured that's the way Elvis would have done it. But he didn't want to make too much racket. He wasn't sure if Elvis might be able to hear that far away.

"Whozzit?" George called.

"Elvis," Ned lied.

He couldn't be sure, but it sounded as if George said, "Crud" before calling out, "Just a minute."

Why did the man need a minute? It was a bungalow. He could have gotten anywhere inside the small structure and still had fifty-eight seconds left to spare.

Ned pressed his ear to the door. He couldn't hear any movement inside.

The lock slid back, and the knob turned. When the door opened, George was looking elsewhere. As he faced Ned, his eyes widened. "Uh-oh," he croaked.

Ned slugged him.

***

"You didn't have to hit him so hard," Donovan said.

Ned rolled George to his belly. He'd already removed the man's gun and his walkie-talkie. Like Paul before him, he didn't carry a wallet. Ned found a foldable knife in George's front pocket and tucked it into his boot.

Travis sat nearby and licked his paw.

"Is he dead?" Sophia bent over with her hands on her knees. She seemed keenly interested in George's fate.

"He's fine," Ned said.

Donovan moved closer. "But he wasn't doing anything."

Ned pulled the duct tape from his pocket. "He would have gone for his gun."

"I don't think so," Sophia said.

Ned noisily stretched a length of tape free. "You don't know what he would have done."

"I agree with her," Donovan said.

Sophia smirked. "We were having a nice conversation."

Ned wrapped the tape around the man's wrists. He continued spinning the tape around George's arms several times. "What were you talking about?"

Sophia motioned toward the unconscious man. "He has an idea for an app."

Ned stretched another piece of duct tape free and started on George's ankles.

"That's a computer program," Donovan said. When Ned didn't respond, he added, "For your phone."

"I know what it is."

"How do we know what you know?" Sophia said. "You're out here in the middle of nowhere. This isn't exactly Silicon Valley."

Ned didn't know where or what Silicon Valley was, but it sounded like a beach in Southern California, although would a beach be in a valley? He pushed the consideration away, and he ripped off the duct tape. He patted it securely around George's ankles. "That should hold him."

He stood and tore a small piece of tape off the roll. He placed it over George's mouth. When he was done, he set the duct tape on the dresser next to George's gun and walkie-talkie.

Ned reached under the bed pillow and pulled out his cell phone. Ned flipped open the phone. He stared at the signal status for a moment.

"Is that a flip phone?" Donovan asked.

Sophia shook her head. "When did you buy that? 1992?"

"Are you getting service?"

Ned ignored the question and snapped it closed. Then he slipped the phone into his pocket. He sat on the edge of his bed and studied the unconscious George. He kicked the man's foot but didn't get a response.

"You sure he's not dead?" Sophia asked.

"He's fine." Ned had slugged him hard, but George was still alive. His body was only processing the sudden damage to his system. His attention shifted to Sophia. "What was this idea you guys were talking about?"

"It was—" she said, but Donovan grabbed her arm and shook his head.

Ned eyed him.

Donovan's smiled with some embarrassment. "It's nothing personal, you know. Just business."

"Maybe I should have left you two here with him."

Donovan and Sophia looked at each other before both shrugged.

"He wasn't any problem for us," Donovan sat on the bed next to Ned. He immediately realized his mistake and stood again.

"George seemed like a nice human," Sophia said. "I'm pretty good at reading people."

Ned cocked his head. "Yeah?"

"I get a sense of people—their essence." Sophia reached for Travis, but the cat darted under the bed. "It radiates out from them."

"This business idea was that good, huh?"

"Better than expected," Sophia said. "What's with that cat?"

"Leave it alone," Donovan said. He excitedly shook a hand at Ned. "The business idea wasn't a home run, but it was definitely a triple."

Sophia's face pinched. "Eh. I wouldn't go that far."

"For sure, a stand-up double."

She shrugged. "Yeah, okay."

"If it's so good," Ned said, "why do you think he told you about it?"

Donovan's eyes darted to the unconscious man. "He didn't say, but I thought it was because he needed start-up financing." Donovan smiled. "That's something I can help with. I mean, I haven't done it before, but I have connections."

Ned motioned to George. "Did he know about your connections?"

"No." Donovan glanced at Sophia. "Did you tell him?"

"I didn't say anything."

Travis poked his head out from under the bed. Sophia reached out for him. The tom trilled and bolted back under the bed.

Ned studied George. "He told you because he wasn't worried."

Donovan's brow furrowed. "I don't understand."

Sophia bolted upright. "Oh my God!"

Ned nodded. "That's right."

"What?" Donovan asked.

Sophia pointed at the fallen man. "He didn't think you could raise the money."

Donovan scowled at George. "That's what he thought?"

Ned waved a hand. "No. That's not it."

Sophia ignored his protest. "If you can't raise the money, you're harmless. I totally misread him."

"*Harmless?*" Donovan crossed his arms and pouted. "I can totally raise that money."

"Sure, you can." Sophia motioned at George. "But that's why he told us. He didn't think you could do it. How could I be so wrong?"

Donovan clucked his tongue. "The

judgmental types are the worst."

"He planned to kill you," Ned said.

Sophia and Donovan stared at each other.

"In the morning. They would keep you alive until then just in case they need a hostage."

Sophia moved next to Donovan. "But he seemed so nice."

Donovan absently scratched his cheek. "Maybe that idea wasn't so good after all. It's an app for buying socks."

Ned didn't own a smartphone or a computer, for that matter, so he couldn't be sure, but it seemed like he'd heard about people using one for that purpose. "Don't people already invest with their phones?"

"*Socks*," Sophia said. "Not *stocks*." She enunciated each word very clearly.

Donovan added. "I didn't realize there were so many different types until he explained it. Like for men, some socks go to the knee, the calf, the mid-calf, and the ankle." Donovan tapped his fingers against those parts of the leg that he identified. "Then there's the crew and quarter length." He looked at Sophia. "But I honestly have no idea what those are, but that's what George said."

She shrugged. "Maybe we did get a little too excited about it at the moment."

"Yeah," Donovan muttered.

"It's not like it's an app for scarves," Sophia said, "because I'm telling you I could use one of those."

George stirred, and his eyelids flickered.

"He's waking," Sophia said. "What should we do?"

"Not promise him any financing," Donovan said. "That's for sure."

Ned thought about dragging George into the bathroom, but that might create a problem if anyone needed to use it. And if he stuffed George into the closet, the man could kick at the door. This bungalow was too far from the next to make noise a true concern, but the sound would be irritating.

Ned could always drag George from the cabin and throw him out into the cold, but that didn't fit his plan to be a better person. He'd already disarmed George and secured him. That's all that was needed for now.

"Keep an eye on him," Ned said. "He's not going anywhere."

Ned considered George's gun for a moment before stuffing it into his coat pocket. He didn't want to leave it inside the bungalow. He slipped the duct tape into the other pocket.

"Forget waiting around," Donovan said to Sophia. "Grab your coat. Let's get out of here."

"What about the cat?" Sophia asked. She bent to look under the bed.

"Hold on," Ned said. "The blizzard is still blowing, and the highway is closed."

"We can make it to Casper," Donovan said.

"But if you don't, no one is coming for you. Not for some time."

Donovan's expression flattened. "What's worse? Dying in a Wyoming blizzard or dying here at the hands of some madmen?"

"But the cat?" Sophia asked.

Ned waved off her question. "Travis is fine." He eyed Donovan. "If you leave now, they'll notice your car is gone."

"So?" Donovan said.

"There are two families staying here. Each of them has a man with a gun guarding them."

Sophia knelt on the ground and looked under the bed. "You think they might do something bad to them if we escape? Come here, kitty kitty."

Ned pointed to the additional walkie-talkie. "Listen to what's happening, but don't pick it up. Don't transmit on it. Understand?" He stepped to the door and opened it. A gust of cold air and snow blew in.

"What are you going to do?" Donovan asked.

"Get the others." Ned stepped into the night.

Chapter 12

Ned stood at the corner of the first bungalow and pressed himself into the building. Across the driveway, the convenience store's rear lights fought gallantly against the falling snow—it was a losing effort. He pulled George's revolver from his pocket. A big stone sat near the edge of the bungalow. Ned lifted the rock and tucked the gun underneath it. The thing now sat cockeyed. It wouldn't fool anyone who looked too closely.

The man Ned had been—the bookkeeper—would never have considered such an action. Leaving behind sidearms was tantamount to death. Had he acted like the man he once was, he would have ripped the gun away from Paul and permanently ended that threat. He would have repeated the action with George. There would be no need for such sneaking.

Now Ned would have to answer for any violent decisions. Marshal Goodspeed seemed an Old Testament sort of woman, so she'd likely support some choices, but it wouldn't make it right for himself. That violence wouldn't make him the person he wanted to be. He would use a gun if he could find no other course of action, but right now, he thought there were other options.

Ned focused on some dim lights that he knew were coming from the second bungalow. Kiki and Brick were in that unit with John. He was too far away for them to see.

He pulled his flip phone from his pocket. The screen glowed bright blue, but the cell signal was weak. He had noticed that a signal had returned while inside the bungalow, but he waited to call until outside for two reasons—he didn't want to give Donavon and Sophia false hope if things didn't result from the call, and he didn't want to expose his secret needlessly.

Ned dialed a number he had memorized. A woman answered after the first ring.

"Horoscope Hook-up," she said. "Helping you find inner peace through a metaphysical love connection. Who is calling?"

"Ned Delahanty," he said softly. Sounds travel at night, although they might not float as far during a blizzard.

A keyboard clicked on the other end of the line.

"Ah, yes," the operator said, "Mr. Delahanty. I see your file right here." It sounded as if she might have tapped a fingernail against a computer screen. The woman inhaled audibly. "Good Lord, sir. You're a frequent caller—" She cut herself off mid-sentence and began counting to herself. "Three, four, five."

Ned whispered, "I can explain—" but the operator interrupted him.

"This isn't a chat line."

"I got that."

"This is for emergency use only." She cleared her throat. "Love emergencies, I mean." She chuckled. "And other connections in the mystic realm."

"Right."

"In other words, this line is for serious hook-ups only."

The U.S. Marshals established the Horoscope Hook-up line for Ned to call in case of an emergency. He wasn't sure if others used the line. The last emergency number was set up under the guise of a vacation planning company, but Ned blew that cover when he contacted it in front of a civilian.

If he ever used the line, he was supposed to act like a customer. This would allow him to use the number even if people were listening in. He and the marshal service would be able to trade information, and supposedly, no one would be the wiser.

There was more keyboard clicking now. The operator said, "I must advise you that this call is being monitored for training purposes."

Ned grunted. "I assumed."

"Sir." She clicked her tongue against the back of her teeth. "There's no need to be snippy."

"Can we get on with it?" Ned glanced around. He whispered, "I'm in a bit of a situation."

The operator spoke louder. "Can you speak up? I can barely hear you."

"That's the problem. I can't speak up."

The operator's voice grew louder now. "Are you having relationship issues with a person nearby?"

"You can say that."

"If you need immediate help, you should call a local authority—someone who can get you out of there quickly. Then you can call us back and update us on the status of your relationship. We could send one of our representatives out to help you. You know, for some one-on-one counseling since you're such a repeat customer."

"I can't call anyone else," Ned said. "There's a blizzard, and the problem is bigger than the weather."

Ned pushed the cell phone tighter against his ear. He heard more keyboard clicking.

"Oh, dear," the woman said. "It does look like a major weather event is occurring in your area." The operator chuckled. "I'm assuming, of course. Based upon your area code."

Ned felt exposed by staying against the side of the building. He was also getting cold. The fingers holding the phone were growing stiff. He didn't want to dance around the coded talk of the Horoscope Hotline any longer. "Get a message to Marshal Goodspeed."

The operator politely laughed. "You're mistaken. No one works here by that name."

"Listen, lady. This is a U.S. Marshal hotline, and I need help."

"Hold, please."

Some dreadful Muzak started. It may have been the most horrible song he'd ever heard. The longer Ned listened, the more convinced he became that it was a synthesized rendition of a song about skyrockets in afternoon flight. One of the girls that hung around the Dawgs used to like seventies music. Ned's former self stopped spending time with her when he learned that.

Ned couldn't believe the U.S. Government's audacity. How dare they subject their informants to an additional level of torture by way of elevator music?

The walkie-talkie in his pocket squelched before broadcasting. *"Hey, Paul?"* Elvis called. *"How are things up there?"*

Ned shook himself free of his thoughts and reached into his pocket. He lifted the radio to his lips. "Bzzkt."

"Your radio is still on the fritz."

"Bzzkt snkrt."

"Did you put new batteries in?"

"Kzzkrt bzzkt skkdhrt."

"I don't understand you. Hey, John?"

The radio squawked. *"Yeah?"*

"Give your radio to Paul. We can't have our watchman being without one."

"Yeah. All right. On my way."

Across the way, additional light spilled out from bungalow two. It didn't take Ned but a second to figure out what caused it.

He snapped the cell phone closed and ran toward the store. He tried his best to stay in the shadows as he went.

***

Ned only had enough time to grab the shovel from inside the store and scoop one line of snow before John rounded the corner. The tall man stopped and eyed him.

"What're you doing?" John asked.

"Safety first," Ned said. He rested the shovel against the building. "And waiting for you."

John stepped back. A wary look entered his eyes. "Why?"

"Paul told me to give you this." He removed the radio from his pocket.

"Where is he?"

"The restroom."

John's brow furrowed. "The restroom is out of order."

"Paul fixed it."

"He did?"

Ned further extended the radio, but John still didn't take it. Instead, he peered into the store. Ned stepped forward, but John noticed the motion and moved back.

"What are you doing?"

Ned waggled the radio. "Don't you want it?"

"Stay where you are."

John stuck his hand into his coat pocket. Ned thought he was reaching for a gun, so he threw the walkie-talkie. The gray brick clunked against the tall man's forehead. John's hand came out of his pocket with his own radio.

Ned clubbed downward onto John's wrist, but the tall man didn't drop the walkie-talkie. Ned reached for John, but the tall man was too quick. He hopped from the sidewalk and sprinted around the corner.

Why had John gone for his radio instead of

his gun?

Ned bent to pick up the walkie-talkie he'd taken from Paul. It came alive in his hand.

"*Elvis!*" John shouted. "*Elvis! We got a problem.*"

***

At the rear edge of the Quik N Go building, Ned attempted to watch the bungalows through the falling snow. The shapes were globs in the darkness with dots of illumination provided by their weak porch lights.

The door to the fourth bungalow opened, and a rectangle of light formed. A figure emerged and moved into the shadow. Ned suspected that to be Elvis.

Communication on the radio had continued briefly after John's excited shout that there was a problem.

Elvis had responded, "*What's going on?*"

"*That clerk—*" John's voice broke from the exertion of running. "*—has Paul's radio.*"

"*Where's Paul?*"

"*I don't know,*" John said.

"*Why didn't you take control of the clerk?*"

There was a pause. "*Uh, because he had a gun.*"

"*Are you sure?*" Elvis asked.

"*Yes. He had a gun. He definitely had a gun.*"

"*Where was your gun?*"

Another pause before John said, "*Uh, he got the drop on me.*"

"You don't sound so sure."

"Believe me. I barely got away."

"All right," Elvis said. *"Go back to your cabin. Let me figure this out."*

The radio went silent after that.

Ned heard that whole radio exchange while inside the Quik N Go. He'd gone there to collect Paul's gun that he'd left under the counter.

Now, he crouched at the back corner of the building. Ned peered into the darkness surrounding bungalow four. That's where he guessed Elvis to be. Was Deputy Lockwood also there? Had Elvis incapacitated him somehow? Maybe the officer was tied up. That's what Ned would have done. Well, the former version of himself, at least. Right now, he'd welcome some law enforcement help.

"Paul," Elvis called through the walkie-talkie.

Ned jumped at the volume of the radio in his pocket. He lowered it.

"Paul, are you there?"

Ned lifted the microphone to his lips and pressed the transmit button. "Bzzkt."

A moment of silence passed in the night. It seemed extra quiet amid the heavy snowfall. Even the wind seemed muted.

"The clerk," Elvis called. Those two words dripped with disgust. *"Is that you?"*

Ned considered responding in the affirmative, but his plan had gone sideways. If John hadn't discovered him, he'd have walked through the bungalows one by one and overpowered each of the crew. He would have devised creative ways to get them to open the doors to their cabins. Maybe it could have been accomplished with a knock. Perhaps he thought it too simple of a plan, but those were often the ones that seemed to work best.

"*Hey, clerk,*" Elvis called, "*I know that's you. Tell me your name again.*"

The element of surprise had vanished. When that happened, the best thing to do was face the problem head-on. He lifted the walkie-talkie and softly spoke. "I'm going to make you a proposition."

"*He speaks. Where's Paul?*"

"If you want to leave in the morning, call your crew to your bungalow."

It didn't broadcast over the radio, but someone laughed in the darkness. Ned could hear the throaty roar from where he stood. It went on for a couple of seconds. Ned searched the snowy night but couldn't find its origin. When the man finished, he loudly cleared his throat.

Elvis said, "*And then what?*"

"I'll let you be."

A figure crossed in front of the light cast by bungalow four. "He'll let me be?" Elvis seemed to be talking to himself. "Who's this guy think he is?" He cleared his voice again before transmitting. "*Well, clerk, I appreciate the generous offer, but I'm going to have to say no.*"

"Or you can leave right now. I won't stop you."

"He won't stop me," Elvis said into the darkness. "Can you believe the arrogance of this guy?" The radio crackled briefly. "*That's not happening either. George?*"

The silence on the air spread for several moments until Elvis repeated. "*George, wake up.*"

Ned lifted the walkie-talkie. "Bzzkt."

Ringo burst into the conversation. "*Elvis, he got George!*"

"*Shut up, Ringo,*" Elvis said. Across the back road, the shadowy figure stood in the lit doorway. "*Clerk, you're not trying to go all John McClane on us, are you?*"

Ned didn't watch a lot of movies, but he understood the reference to the movie *Die Hard*.

"*Because we're not going down that easy,*" Elvis said.

"*Suit yourself.*"

"*Bring it on, clerk. Yippee-ki-yay—*"

Ned fired the revolver at the cabin.

"Hey!" Elvis cried and jumped inside. The door slammed shut behind him.

The radio chirped before Ringo asked, "*Who's firing?*"

"*It's the clerk,*" Elvis said. "*He's got a gun.*"

"*He's coming for us,*" John transmitted.

"*Everyone stay off the radio,*" Elvis said. "*He's listening.*"

John asked, "*Should I go after George?*"

The radio squelched before Elvis responded. "*John, what'd I say? Stay where you are. I'll come to you in a minute. Let me figure this out.*"

"*Yeah, John,*" Ringo added. In the background, Alden and Hattie's children squealed. *"Take a pill, will ya? I can't believe how you get so worked up over the littlest things. It's just one shot. It's not that big of a deal. And think of how many of us there are."* The Fodey children playfully screeched. *"Hey, will you keep those kids quiet? I'm trying to have a conversation over here. What was I saying? Yeah, so John, we've got the guy way outnumbered."*

Elvis stepped out of his cabin and yelled, *"Stop transmitting, Ringo!"*

The radio went silent.

"Ringo?" Elvis said. Even though he tried to sound calm, his voice was obviously strained.

"Yeah?"

"Stay off the radio."

Ned ran toward the front of the building. When he passed the corner, he sprinted deeper into the parking lot. The snow was deep now, and he lifted his feet high to clear the powder. He continued until he stood at the unlit pylon sign. The lower portion announced the vacant rooms—

Available bungalows for rent! Cheap!

There was enough ambient light to see what he needed to do. Ned yanked out four letters and an exclamation point. His eyes darted over the remaining letters. He quickly settled on a word and pulled out seven more letters and the second exclamation point. Then he swiped the remaining letters away from the sign; they fell silently to the ground.

Ned rearranged the remaining letters into a

new, more important message—*Help! Robbers!*

He stepped around to the other side and repeated the action. When he was done, he paused to admire his work. Would anyone see it since the panel was unlit? And if they did, would they believe the message and actually get help?

Those were two big questions.

Ned stopped staring at his literary accomplishment and darted to the far edge of the convenience store.

Chapter 13

The snowfall intensified amid the gusting winds. Ned sprinted as fast as he could along the front of the building. When he rounded the far corner of the store, he stepped into the deep snow again. He shoved the gun into his right coat pocket.

Water hadn't seeped through his leather boots, but his feet were cold, nonetheless. He made big leaping jumps as he hurried along the side of the building. When he neared the rear corner, he paused long enough to ensure that none of the crew were moving about. He couldn't see very far in the falling snow, but it seemed a worthwhile precaution. Ned sprinted through a halo of light at the back of the building as he crossed the road toward the first bungalow.

He listened intently to the radio in the event someone saw him, but no calls were issued forth. Ned entered the shadows again and was about to pass his truck when something caught his eye. He paused near the rear tire and squatted. Ned ran his fingers over the rubber to make sure.

A puncture wound was in the sidewall of the tire. The snow was so high that he almost missed that it was flat. His cold fingers touched the hole. Still squatting, he shuffled forward and used the truck to conceal his movements.

Ned found a puncture in the front tire as well. Someone had disabled his rig. One flat tire is only a temporary delay. Most cars have a spare. It would be an inconvenience and waste some time, but the truck could be serviceable soon enough. But two flat tires put a vehicle out of commission until help could arrive.

He crept around the front of the truck. The snow drifted against the plow's blade as if daring it to be pushed away. The powder went above his calf when Ned stepped into the small snow drift. He held onto the metal blade until he made it to the nearby Land Rover.

The night was darker between the two vehicles. Ned felt along the Land Rover's front tire's side until he found another puncture. He shuffled awkwardly through the snow to the vehicle's rear to satisfy his suspicions. The puncture on the back tire was easier to find.

Were the tires punctured before he subdued George, and he simply missed them? Or had someone disabled the vehicle afterward and freed George? If they had been punctured before then, that meant he missed this detail. Perhaps he'd been too focused on getting to the first bungalow and hadn't suspected the crew might do such a thing.

And if they had freed the man, should he go back inside to check on Donovan and Sophia? Arguments could be made to do such a thing, but he wanted to press on.

Ned peered around the back of the Land Rover. He couldn't see much through the gusting snow. He reasoned if he couldn't see them, then they couldn't see him. He stood into a crouch and ran for the second bungalow.

His strides were awkward—knees high with boots pulling heavily out of the fallen snow. The cold air bit into his lungs even though his breath was shallow and ragged. The exertion was far more than he expected.

Ned's foot caught on something hidden under the powder. He stumbled for several steps before sprawling headfirst into the deep snow. Wet, cold powder found its way into his coat and down his shirt. Ned righted himself and brushed the snow from his face.

He needed to get out of the wide open and behind some cover. Even though it was dark, and the falling snow was thick, he might be seen. All it would take is an errant flashlight beam from a nosy crew member to spot him. Ned took two steps and stopped. The weight in his right pocket felt wrong, and he patted it. The gun was gone, but the walkie-talkie remained in his left pocket.

Ned spun and looked at where he'd fallen. For a moment, he considered going back to search for the revolver. John had reported to everyone that he had a gun. They would all expect him to be armed now. As much as he didn't want to carry a weapon anymore, he'd created a situation where it seemed smarter to do so. And he admitted that the revolver felt comfortable in his hand. It would certainly level the playing field now that he'd lost the element of surprise.

The last thing he wanted was to be discovered digging through the snow while on his hands and knees. He knew what would happen then. It was better to press on. He spun and ran toward Brick's Ford Raptor.

Ned crouched next to the front tire. His fingers were stiff from the cold, but they quickly found a puncture wound. If there was one, he knew there would be a second. He didn't bother searching further.

He cupped his hands and blew on them. A mist of white air passed through his fingers and gave him temporary relief. He blew again.

Ned hurried to the front of the bungalow. He quickly reached up and unscrewed the bulb. The hot surface stung his frozen fingers.

He pressed his ear against the door. Ned expected to hear loud voices. With the recent gunfire, shouting could have been expected. But Ned could barely hear anything. Perhaps there were murmurs inside, but that might have been a trick of the howling wind.

Ned raised his hand to knock but stopped. He stepped back and prepared to kick the door. He hesitated once more. He reached out and gently turned the doorknob.

A heavy sigh greeted him when he stepped inside. No one noticed him initially. John sat on the edge of the bed with his head in his hands. Brick and Kiki stood near him.

"We're going to die," John said. The tall man stared at the ground.

Brick leaned over to get a look at John's face.

"You really think so?"

"I've got a lot to live for," Kiki said. She tapped her sternum. "My followers count on me."

Ned cleared his throat.

She turned and faced him. "You?"

John's head popped up. "Him!"

Brick's eyes widened. "Dude."

As John stood, Ned leaped forward and hit him with his elbow. John stiffened and fell back onto the bed.

Kiki and Brick jumped clumsily away.

Ned pulled the gun from John's waistband.

Brick leaned over the unconscious man and shook his shoulder. "You didn't have to do that."

"He had a gun."

"He wasn't going for it."

Kiki moved next to her boyfriend. "Brick is right." She leaned over John. "The guy was sort of sweet."

"Sweet?" Ned said. "Are you kidding me?"

The walkie-talkie on the nightstand crackled. "*Everybody check-in,*" Elvis said. "*Ringo?*"

She responded quickly. "*I'm here and a-okay, thanks for asking. Can someone come and relieve me or trade posts or something? You know how I am with kids. They're giving me a headache something fierce. Do you hear that?*" The radio picked up the playful screaming of four little girls. "*It's like being inside a madhouse or a jet engine or something. I don't know.*" Ringo turned away from the radio's speaker and yelled, "*Would you guys knock it off?*" When her voice returned to the regular level, she said,

"They won't listen to their parents any more than they'll listen to me. How come no one is responding? Oh right. Sorry." She stopped transmitting.

"Ringo," Elvis said very calmly.

"Yes?"

"How many times do I have to tell you?"

"Short responses. Got it."

The radio squelched before Elvis said, *"John, check-in."*

Brick and Kiki looked from the unconscious man to Ned.

"What are you going to do?" Kiki asked.

Ned grabbed the walkie-talkie from the nightstand. "Bzzkt."

"He got John!" Ringo shouted.

"I know that," Elvis said. *"Stay off the radio."*

"Well, that means it's just us now," Ringo said. *"What do you think? Should we go after him? Instead of waiting for him to pick us off like roadkill— although that's not how roadkill gets got, is it? Anyway, you get my point. I'm thinking we should get together and go after him. What do you say? I'm just itchin' to get out of here and leave these kids behind."* The girls shrieked with laughter. *"So what do you say? Oh, right."*

The radio went silent.

Ned closed the bungalow's door and locked it.

"Elvis?" Ringo called. *"Hello? Why are you ignoring me?"*

"They might be coming," Ned said. "You should get in the bathroom and stay out of the way."

Brick and Kiki hurried around the corner.

Ned knelt on the floor and held the gun ready in case someone burst through the door. "There's five of them in the crew."

Brick poked his head out of the bathroom. "John told us. Elvis and the Beatles, huh?"

"I took out George and Paul already."

"Took them out?" Brick asked.

Now, Kiki's head appeared over Brick's shoulder. "As in permanently forever?"

Ned didn't take his eyes off the door. "No. They're tied up."

"Maybe they've gotten free," Brick said.

"I doubt it. Ringo just said it was the two of them. I don't think they've rescued the others yet."

"Why not?" Kiki asked.

"They're tied up with responsibilities. Ringo's guarding a family, and Elvis is guarding a deputy."

"A deputy?" Brick and Kiki said simultaneously.

The radio squawked once. Ringo said, "*Hey, Elvis, if you're going after the clerk, can I go? I think I finally understand cabin fever. So, maybe we can sneak over there and catch him when he walks out.*"

When she stopped transmitting, Elvis said, "*Ringo!*"

"*What? What did I do now?*"

Ned lifted the radio. "Thank you, Ringo."

"*You see?*" Elvis transmitted. "*You see what you did? This is what I'm talking about. I should*" *have left you in Kansas."*

"That was uncalled for," Ringo said. *"I'm like the most loyal person you got. Okay, maybe Paul. But after him, I'm definitely the most loyal. And maybe if you gave me more responsibility than watching these kids, I wouldn't be trying to get your attention so much."*

Ned set the gun and radio down. "You can come out now," he called to Brick and Kiki.

"Oh, for crying out loud," Elvis said, *"we're not doing this."*

"If not now," Ringo said, *"when? This seems a good time to me since I'm not doing anything but standing here listening to this—"* The Fodey children shouted.

Ned lowered the radio's volume and handed it to Brick. "If the radio chatter stops, we need to listen for someone coming to the door." He reached into his pocket for the roll of duct tape.

"What are you going to do with that?" Kiki asked.

Ned motioned toward John. "I'm going to tie him up."

"Is that really necessary? He was very nice to us."

Ned's eyes narrowed. "Didn't he destroy your cell phones?"

Kiki's head bobbled. "Yeah, maybe taping him up isn't such a bad idea."

Ned grabbed John's hands and wrapped tape around them. The roll repeatedly snicked as he tugged and yanked. When he was done, he ripped the silver tape off.

John stirred, and his eyes blinked. Ned yanked him upright by his shirt. "Gonna cause me any problems?"

"No."

"See?" Kiki said. "We told you he was nice."

Ned knelt. "Put your ankles together."

John did so.

"What's your deal?" Ned asked. He started a piece of tape and hooked it to one of John's ankles. "You don't seem as enthusiastic as Paul or Ringo."

John shrugged. "I'm not."

Ned wrapped the tape around John's legs. "Then why do it?"

"Sometimes you do things you don't want to do." John leaned down to make eye contact with Ned. "Has that ever happened to you?"

Kiki slapped Brick's arm. "Set up the camera. Hurry up."

Ned was about to tell her no, but figured what was it going to hurt now? If he made it out of here alive, he'd leave this location. He couldn't stay here.

Ned ripped the duct tape and patted the last bit onto the man's legs.

"How long have you been robbing banks?"

"For a few weeks," John absently said. He watched Brick rummage through his bag.

"What are you waiting for?" Ned said. "Keep going."

"I thought maybe we should wait." John lifted his chin toward Brick. "Until they're set up."

Brick removed a small camera from the bag

along with a tripod. He glanced at Ned and John. "This'll only take a minute." He expertly extended a three-legged stand, then settled the camera onto it. Once the items were connected, Brick moved behind Ned. "I think this is the best spot. And... we're rolling."

John eyed Ned. "Start over."

"What?"

"Ask your question again so they can get it on camera." John eyed Kiki. "I can't wait to see your channel. You two seem very sweet."

Kiki beamed, then her gaze shifted to Ned. "I told you he was nice."

"The colors and shadows are great," Brick muttered. "Very mysterious." He fiddled with the camera.

"Go ahead," John said to Ned. "I'll act like I'd never heard your question before."

"What's your deal?" Ned asked. It was an unenthusiastic repeat of his earlier question.

John's eyes widened. "My deal?" He turned his face away from the camera as if lost in thought.

Kiki shooed Ned to ask his next question.

Ned almost robotically asked, "How long have you been robbing banks?"

A sad smile spread across John's face. "That's the question, isn't it?"

Chapter 14

"Confession is supposed to be good for the soul." John's eyes narrowed. "Been a long time since I've had to do such a thing."

"You're stalling," Ned said. He grabbed the walkie-talkie from his pocket and stood. The volume was low, and he held it to his ear. It sounded as if Elvis and Ringo were still bickering.

"I'm easing myself into it." John glanced to Kiki and Brick, then returned his attention to Ned. "You see, I didn't want to do this—any of it. You got to understand Elvis is very convincing. He has ways of getting what he wants."

"What's his real name?" Ned asked.

John looked down for a moment. Then he glanced at the camera. "I'd rather not say."

Ned balled his free hand into a fist, and his face warmed. His former self, the bookkeeper, would have forced the man to spill the truth by now. He wouldn't have let John dole it out in a slow dribble like he was doing.

But Ned didn't want to be that man and do those things. Part of being a better person was suffering through moments like this. He relaxed his hand, inhaled deeply, and asked, "Why not? Why wouldn't you rather say?"

"Maybe in a moment." John looked at Ned.

"I'm having second thoughts about the camera."

"They can turn it off." Ned would be happier if it was.

"No," John said. "I'm sure I'll get over it. I just need another minute."

This was taking too long. Ned balled his hand. A well-placed punch across the chin would loosen the truth like a spigot on a hot summer day.

"What about you?" Kiki asked. "What's your name?"

"Yeah," Brick said. "And the others with you."

Ned relaxed slightly. With the camera on, it seemed that Kiki and Brick assumed the roles of interviewers.

"I'll tell you my name—" John considered the camera. "In a minute. As for the others—" He shrugged. "I don't know."

"What don't you know?" Brick asked.

"I don't know their names."

Kiki threw her arms in the air. "How can't you know? We need names." She repeatedly slapped the back of her hand into the palm of the other. "The Kikinators aren't going to stick around on a video if they don't get the payoff. Right now, you're totally giving us clickbait."

Ned had no idea what she was talking about.

"I would tell you their names if I knew," John said. "I promise. I hold no allegiance to them." He held his duct-taped hands over his heart.

"They're not your friends?" Brick asked.

"No."

Kiki waved her hands. "How is that even

possible?"

John scoffed. "We've only known each other for a few days. Some less than the others."

Ned lifted the radio to his ear. Elvis and Ringo were still arguing.

"How can that be?" Kiki asked. She walked around like a prosecuting attorney asking questions. "You're robbing banks."

Brick clucked his tongue to get her attention. His focus remained on the camera's video screen. He motioned for her to move back into the frame. Kiki started as if she realized she had wasted an opportunity and quickly moved back near John. She straightened and repeated her question. "But how can that be? You're robbing banks."

"I was second into the group,' John said. "The first was Paul. And that's exactly how Elvis introduced us when they showed up at my place of employment. Paul, this is John and vice versa." He waved his duct-taped hands back and forth. "Elvis didn't give us a chance to pick our code names or anything—he just assigned them. That's how it was."

"Did you like the code names?" Kiki asked.

John shrugged. "I didn't care. At least, he didn't give us ones based on colors like Mr. Pink or Mr. Black. I would have hated something like that. Plus, imagine walking around calling Paul, Mister Anything. That would have gone straight to his big fat head."

"Tell us your name," Kiki said.

John stared into the camera. "Not yet."

"Why? Is it because we can't handle the truth?" Kiki clapped her hands and stomped a foot with each word.

"Huh?" John asked.

Brick stiffened and looked over the camera. "What are you doing?"

She eyed him. "I saw it in a movie once."

"Not like that."

Kiki crossed her arms. "I'm doing the best I can. I've never interrogated anyone before."

"You're doing fine," John said.

She smiled. "Thank you."

"This is the nicest interrogation I've ever experienced. Please proceed."

Kiki asked, "Why won't you tell us your name?"

He paused for a moment as he considered the camera. "I can give you a name, but it won't mean anything. And it's been so long since I've said my real one that I'm not sure if I even believe it's mine anymore."

Ned lowered the walkie-talkie from his ear. "Cut the camera."

Brick turned his head. "Excuse me?"

Kiki frowned. "You've got to be joking."

Ned pointed at the camera. "Now." His expression hardened.

Brick's fingers fumbled over the camera. "Take it easy, fella."

He pointed at Brick's walkie-talkie. "Start listening to that."

"What for?"

"Just do it. And go over there." Ned lifted his

chin toward the far corner of the room. "If the radio chatter changes or it sounds like they're headed this way, let me know."

"Who made you boss?" Kiki asked.

Ned scowled.

Brick handed Kiki the radio and pulled her closer to him.

She said, "The Kikinators have a right to know what's going on!"

"Kiki," Brick said, "not now."

"But we were just getting to the good stuff."

Ned knelt next to the bed and eyed John. He whispered, "What's the deal?"

"I've got a situation."

"How long have you been in this situation?"

John said, "Six years."

"What got you into this situation?"

"Are you asking what I was arrested for?"

Ned shook his head. "How'd you get into the program?"

John stared at him.

"Listen, you're about to go on the internet with your story, so you might as well give it to me straight. Everyone in the world is going to know who you are."

"I should have kept my fat mouth shut." John ruefully shook his head. "I talked to the feds about things I had no business talking about."

"You ratted."

John winced. "Yeah."

"Where did they put you?"

"Corral City, Texas. Population twenty-seven.

You don't know what living in a small town is like."

"Who's Elvis to you?"

John lifted his gaze. "He was the man sworn to protect me."

Ned abruptly stood. He studied John for several seconds before saying, "He was your witness inspector."

"Yeah." John's eyes narrowed. "After I got placed, I never heard from him again. A new inspector arrived and took over my case. I thought everything was fine. Well, as fine as living in Corral City could be. Then Elvis showed up with Paul, and everything went off the rails."

"What'd he say?"

"Can I stand?"

"No."

"I'm sort of uncomfortable being all tied up."

"I can put tape over your mouth and stuff you in the closet."

John's gaze drifted toward the ceiling. After a moment, he said, "Elvis showed up and said my file was compromised and he needed to move me."

"You didn't think that was weird with him not being your inspector anymore?"

"But he used to be."

"And what did he say about Paul?"

"He said his file was compromised, too. That's why the code names. He didn't want either of us knowing too much about the other."

"What happened then?"

"We robbed a liquor store in Denton, a town

just north of Corral City. He said we needed some off-the-books money. That's when I knew things weren't as they seemed."

"Why didn't you try to get away?"

"Because Paul went willingly. He didn't know what Elvis was doing any more than I did, but he was all about it. It seemed to me that he'd had enough of hiding."

"Then you picked up the others?"

John extended his hands. "You sure you won't let me loose?"

"No."

His hands dropped into his lap. "Elvis picked up George in Depew, Oklahoma. I would have given anything to be assigned there. I think there were almost five hundred people. That's the big time compared to where I was."

Ned's thoughts drifted for a moment. He imagined Marshals Onderdonk and Goodspeed violating the trust he placed in them. While he wasn't a fan of law enforcement, he had grown strangely fond of those two.

Kiki broke Ned's thoughts by lifting her hand and wiggling the radio. "They stopped talking."

Ned faced her. "Did they say anything about heading in this direction?"

"Not that I heard."

Brick shrugged. "I wasn't paying attention."

Ned raised his eyebrows.

"But I will now." Brick pointed at the silent walkie-talkie. "If anyone says anything. I'll let you know."

Ned eyed John. "So the three of you were in

Depew. What happened then?"

"We robbed a couple more places."

"Had you done that before?"

"You mean, is that what I got arrested for in the first place? No. I was just a bouncer in a club. That's it. Nothing fancy. I saw some things I shouldn't have, but I kept it all to myself. Then the cops busted me with a little coke." John's head bounced from side to side. "Maybe more than a little. Anyway, I got kicked up to the feds, who offered me a deal in exchange for no prison. It seemed like a no-brainer."

"Once you realized what was going on with Elvis, why not tell him no? Why rob and steal with him?"

"He said if I didn't agree, he'd sell my whereabouts to my former boss."

"And you believed him?"

"Hard not to after he showed me a website that had my picture on it. Also had these other pictures of me with what I'd look like with different haircuts and hair colors." He wiped his hands over his mouth. "That's an unsettling thing to see, let me tell you."

Ned knew it was. He'd seen the same thing during his first assignment. Viewing pictures of himself with different haircuts and colors had been troubling. But most unnerving was seeing his name under the banner of FBI Rat.

"I figured," John said, "that I'd rather be alive and committing crimes with some psycho U.S. marshal than dead with a clean conscience. I'm weak that way."

Ned scratched his chin. "When did you get Ringo?"

"We picked her up in Tyro, Kansas. You notice how much she talks? I think it's probably because she was in that town for so long. She probably didn't have anyone to speak with."

"When did you start robbing banks?"

"Right after Elvis picked up Ringo. I think she was the final piece in his puzzle."

"What's the master plan?"

John shrugged. "Elvis never said there was one, but we came to Wyoming so he could meet up with—"

Kiki interrupted. "They're coming." She lifted the radio. "They just said."

"Just like that?" Ned said.

She nodded. "Just like that." Kiki lowered her voice, speaking in baritone. "'Let's go get him.'"

"I heard it, too," Brick said. He pointed at the walkie-talkie. "Like she said."

"Turn it up," Ned said. He eyed John. "Does that sound right? He knows we're listening, so why announce that they're coming?"

John shrugged. "He's crafty. You can't trust him."

"Turn off the lights," Ned said.

Brick flicked the switches, and the bungalow went mostly dark. Only a single nightlight remained.

Ned moved to the front of the bungalow. He carefully pushed a curtain away from a window.

Outside, a man stood near Brick's truck. A gun dangled in his hand. He lifted a radio to his lips. *"C'mon outside, clerk. We've got some talking to do."*

Ned let the curtain fall into place.

"We've got the place surrounded."

Unless Elvis had somehow freed Paul or George, that left only Ringo to help. Claiming that the bungalow was surrounded was a bit of an exaggeration.

Ned stepped toward the middle of the room and paused. Although, what if Elvis had rescued George and Paul? Could they be out there now? It was possible, but it seemed like it would have taken more time to get the two men. But if they were outside now, then boasting that the building was surrounded wasn't an exaggeration at all.

There was no rear window for Ned to refute that claim, so he had to assume someone was standing there. Most likely, it would be Ringo in any scenario.

Ned checked one of the side windows. He couldn't see anything outside except more snowy darkness. Bungalow three was in the distance. That was the unit he believed to be empty.

The radio squawked. Elvis said, *"I'm gonna give you the count of two—"*

"Not three?" Kiki asked.

"—then we're coming in."

In the bungalow's darkness, Ned could barely see Brick. "Do you have an alarm on your truck?" he asked.

"You bet." It sounded as if Brick were

grinning. "I got a Rockford Fosgate in there. You think I'd leave that baby unprotected?"

"*One*," Elvis said.

Ned grabbed the walkie-talkie in his pocket. "Hold on," he said. "I'm coming out."

"*I knew there was something off about you, clerk.*"

Ned said to Brick, "When I tell you to, hit that alarm."

"Yeah. Okay."

Ned patted his pocket to reassure himself that he still had John's gun. Then he lifted the window. A rush of wind, snow, and cold poured into the small room.

"I'm coming out," Ned said into the walkie-talkie. He then tucked the radio back into his coat pocket.

"You ought to be careful," John said. "That man aims to do you harm."

Kiki and Brick came closer.

"Are you sure you want to do this?" Brick asked.

"Should we film it?" Kiki said. "The Kikinators would love this. It's so intense."

John stood with some difficulty due to his duct-taped ankles. "I never told you his name."

"What more do I need to know besides he's a marshal?"

Brick and Kiki eyed each other. "A marshal?" they said in unison.

"His name is Titus Grizzle," John said. "If we all make it out alive, it would be great if he saw justice."

The radio squawked from inside Ned's pocket. *"Taking your sweet time, aren't you, clerk?"*

Ned turned off the radio and moved to the window. "When he comes in here, you tell him I held you hostage. Whatever you got to tell him, you do it. Understand?"

"We understand," Brick said.

"I'm happy to blame it all on you," Kiki added.

Ned put his hands on the window ledge. "Hit the alarm."

A loud piercing shrill rang out from the front of the bungalow, and a gun fired.

Ned dove through the window.

Chapter 15

Ned's leap through the window wasn't graceful. A man of his size jumping through anything wouldn't be. His head and shoulders made it through the opening before his knees hit the windowsill with an unexpected thunk. The world quickly upended itself.

He flailed his arms as his head went toward the snowy ground. His feet went skyward, which caused his knees to act as a fulcrum. He briefly teetered until he slid through the window, his legs dragging against the exterior windowsill until he landed in a snowy heap.

Ned stared into the night sky as snowflakes drifted down like the white fuzz from a TV screen. A shrieking alarm rang out through the night.

"Turn that thing off!" Titus 'Elvis' Grizzle yelled. "Turn it off now, or I'm coming in shooting."

Ned pulled the gun from his pocket, rolled to his hands and knees, then stood.

The alarm silenced and an eerie quiet fell over the bungalows.

"What the heck was that about?" Grizzle asked.

Ned sprinted through the darkness. Crossing the open field to the third bungalow was a difficult journey. The snow was calf-high now, and he hurt from crashing through the window. He'd never been in a blizzard before and was surprised at how fast the snow fell.

He expected a shot to ring out, but so far, none had come.

Each step required Ned to lift his knees so high that his boots could clear the snow.

A ringing started, and Ned immediately dropped a hand to cover the cell phone hidden in his pocket. He glanced over his shoulder in the direction of the road. Due to the blizzard, he could barely see anything.

Grizzle yelled, "Hey! Someone's in the field."

A shot rang out, and Ned crouched. He didn't stop running, though. The final twenty feet to the third bungalow was excruciating in this contorted stance. Getting his feet up high enough to clear the powder was difficult.

The cell phone rang again, quickly followed by two more gunshots.

Ned dove into the snow and crawled behind the third bungalow. He righted himself and peeked around the corner. A shadowy figure stomped its way toward him. Ned took careful aim and fired.

Grizzle dropped into the snow.

It took great care to get the bullet close to the former marshal without hitting him.

"That's the only warning shot you get," Ned yelled. "After that, I'm putting you in the ground."

Grizzle lifted his head. "A warning?"

"You heard me, but I could have taken your

head off. Go back to your bungalow."

The cell phone rang again, and Ned pulled it out. He flipped it open.

"Hello, Mr. Delahanty. This is Amy with Psychic Outreach."

"This isn't a good time," Ned said.

He peeked around the corner to keep an eye on Grizzle. The man lay on the ground, but his head kept popping up like one of those Whack-a-Mole games.

"I'll make it quick," Amy said, "As you may know, Psychic Outreach is affiliated with Horoscope Hook-up."

Ned *did* know. This wing of the U.S. Marshal's emergency contact system had called him previously while he posed as a mall Santa Claus.

Grizzle pushed himself to his hands and feet.

"Quicker," Ned said.

Amy cleared her throat. "Well, yes. We noticed a call from your number, and I thought you might need a reading."

"I'm in a situation here."

Amy chuckled. "Aren't we all? It says here you're a Libra, is that correct?"

Grizzle stood but remained hunched. He awkwardly backpedaled through the deep snow. His gun pointed into the darkness. Soon, he became a shadowy figure in the falling snow.

"Titus Grizzle," Ned said.

"I'm not sure what that is." There was some keyboard clicking. "Is that some sort of chakra cleansing— Oh my. Hold the line."

Grizzle's shadow waved for someone to advance up the other side of the bungalow. Ned kept the phone to his ear and hurried along the back of the building to the opposite corner.

It had to be Ringo sneaking up to get him. Or perhaps the marshal had freed Paul or George.

To peek around the opposite corner, he put the gun into his left hand and held the phone in his right. It wasn't optimal, but it prevented Ned from exposing too much of himself around the corner.

Halfway up the building, crouched with his gun at the ready, was Deputy Lockwood. When he noticed Ned, the officer yelled, "I got him, Titus!"

A shot rang out through the night.

Ned fired back, and the deputy dove into the snow. He tried to shoot the man. This was no time for a warning shot, but firing left-handed wasn't his specialty.

He turned and ran along the back of the building. Ned expected Grizzle to have advanced again, yet he figured it was the least dangerous choice. Running toward the last bungalow put him closer to Ringo and the Fodey family. He made the tactical decision to run through Grizzle and get back to the first couple of bungalows which seemed like safer territory.

Ned traipsed awkwardly through the snow along the rear of the bungalow. He didn't pause as he burst into the open field. He raised his gun and fired in the direction of Grizzle.

The marshal was halfway up the building's

length, but he lunged for the ground.

Ned squeezed the trigger a couple of times as he ran through the snow. He didn't expect to hit Grizzle. He was still shooting with his left hand, running, and blindly aiming backward. Hitting a man with that type of shot was akin to shooting an arrow in the sky and hitting a squirrel on its descent.

Racing across the open field the second time wasn't nearly as difficult as the first due to the adrenaline surging in Ned's veins. When he arrived at the second cabin, he pressed his back against it and stole a glance in Grizzle's direction.

The snowfall made it difficult to see the man, but no shadowy figures advanced toward him. Ned tossed the empty gun to the ground and lifted the phone to his ear.

"—gunfire?" Amy asked.

"Grizzle and his crew have taken civilian hostages."

"What about you?"

"He hasn't succeeded in that yet."

"What are they after?"

"I don't know."

There was some clacking on the keyboard. "We're working on some help, but it appears we've got a problem."

Ned looked up into the falling snow.

"Due to the weather, it's going to take some time to get there."

"We may not have that much time," Ned said.

A shadowy figure emerged from the snowy

ground. Grizzle took a couple of tentative steps toward Ned.

"Stay positive, Mr. Delahanty. Your horoscope is good today. It says you'll succeed by avoiding hasty—"

He snapped his phone shut.

Grizzle stepped forward again and righted himself fully. "I think he's out of ammo!"

From a distance, Deputy Lockwood asked, "Are you sure?"

"Yeah." A few seconds passed before he added, "Of course."

"Then go get him!" Lockwood shouted. "He almost took off my head."

Ned pulled the radio from his pocket. He keyed it and said, "Hey, Titus."

Silence fell over the night. It stayed that way for several beats.

"How's he know your name?" Lockwood shouted.

The radio buzzed before Grizzle responded. *"What do you want?"*

Ned lifted the walkie-talkie to his lips. "They know." He peeked around the corner to watch the marshal. The darkness and the snow made it difficult to see any facial expressions, but it was clear the man had stepped backward.

The radio squawked a bit when Ringo jumped on. *"Who knows? What's he talking about, Elvis? And if he knows your name, do we still have to use these stupid nicknames? You know, I never really liked being Ringo, although it was the coolest name in the bunch. Oh, right. Sorry."*

Ned keyed the radio. "The marshals know, Ringo. They know Titus is here, and they're on the way."

"*How do they know?*" Ringo asked. Her voice rose with panic. "*Does that mean they'll know you were behind all those jobs?*"

"Lockwood," Grizzle yelled into the night, "get over here!"

Ringo continued chattering on the radio. "*And if they know about the jobs, will they know who all helped? I mean, like each of us? Because I came in late, you know.*"

"Stop transmitting!" Grizzle shouted. He ran toward the back road.

"*I wasn't a full participant,*" Ringo said. "*I only went along to get along—you know? Like that's how it is when you're late to the party.*"

Grizzle disappeared into the darkness.

Ned didn't know when the snow would let up. Even if it did, the roads wouldn't clear any time soon. He'd have to survive, but that likely couldn't be done alone. Not since Grizzle was working with Deputy Lockwood and Ringo. Ned would need some help.

He ran along the back of the bungalow. When he came to the next open field, he sprinted to the nearest structure. He crept along its side and stopped near the front. He flipped up the big rock and picked up the gun. It felt good in his hand, which made him feel sort of bad. It was something a better man shouldn't feel good about.

Ned knocked on the front door. "It's me," he

said, "the clerk."

Brick opened the door. "We heard shooting."

"You survived," John said.

"It would have been better if we were filming," Kiki said. "No one will believe it."

Ned shut the door. "The deputy is working with them."

"What?" Brick said.

"Ah, man." Kiki flicked her hand. "That's terrible. The Kikinators would have loved that twist."

John eyed her disapprovingly. "Where are they now?"

"They've gone to get Ringo," Ned said.

"What for?" Brick asked.

John jerked his head to the walkie-talkie in the unit. "Probably so she'll stop transmitting." Ringo continued to chatter on the radio. "Are the marshals really on the way?"

Ned nodded. "I called them."

"You have service?" Kiki asked. She threw her hands in the air. "And we don't have our phones! Could this day get any worse?"

Brick's eyes narrowed. "Why did you call the marshals instead of the cops?"

Ned eyed John. "You've got a choice to make—either run with them or help us."

"At this point, it's no question. I'm with you."

Ned reached into his boot and pulled out the knife. He knelt and cut the tape surrounding John's ankles, then his hands. "When you get in trouble," Ned said, "what kind of set-up did they give you to call?"

"It's been the same all these years—a polling station. I'm supposed to call in and pretend I want to take a survey. Why? What do they have you call?"

"Doesn't matter." Ned handed John his phone. "You should call. Tell them what's going on. You're at the Quik N Go in Eagle's Feet, Wyoming."

John nodded once, then flipped it open.

Kiki hurried over to marvel at the cell phone. "Why don't you just use smoke signals?"

Ned stood and moved toward the door.

Brick asked, "Where are you going?"

"We should all go to the first bungalow."

"We?" Brick asked.

"We need to stick together."

"But *we* didn't do anything," Kiki said.

Ned put his hand on the doorknob. "I'm not forcing you to do anything, but if Grizzle and the deputy come back, they're gonna hold you hostage. They're running out of bargaining tools, especially once the marshals arrive."

Brick glanced at Kiki. Without further word, they both grabbed their coats.

Ned's eyes lowered for a minute, lost in thought.

John moved over and handed Ned his phone back. "They said they're aware of the situation and that help is already on the way." He glanced at Brick and Kiki as they zipped up their gear. "What's going on?"

"Can I trust you to lead these people to the first bungalow and wait for me until I get there?"

"What are you going to do?"

"Can I trust you?"

John nodded.

"Then let's move." He yanked open the door, and the cold blasted in. Snow blew over the transom. Ned stepped outside, and the others followed. He pointed in the direction of the first bungalow. John led Kiki and Brick away. The three of them were soon enveloped by the falling snow and disappeared into the darkness.

Ned hunched and ran in the opposite direction.

***

When Ned neared the third bungalow, he paused long enough to consider his options. He didn't think anyone was inside, especially since no vehicles were parked out in front. He believed he knew where everyone now was. Ringo had been in the fifth bungalow with Alden and Hattie's family, while Grizzle and Lockwood were in the fourth.

But that didn't mean people couldn't have changed their locations, and that didn't mean Grizzle and Lockwood weren't out roaming in the cold for him. That seemed unlikely as the weather was terrible. It was likely they had gathered back in the fourth bungalow to develop a plan.

Fortune favored the bold. He'd read that on an old Marine's tattoo once, and he liked its sentiment. He charged through the snowy darkness and raced quietly past the third bungalow. His boots felt heavy with snow.

When he cleared the middle building, he continued the frantic pace. The cold air bit into his lungs. He lost his footing once and stumbled. He didn't fall but did slow his gait.

Outside the fourth structure, Ned leaned against the rear of the white Chevy van. Through the howling wind, he struggled to hear voices from inside the bungalow. It was a futile attempt, but he tried, nonetheless.

He pulled the knife from his boot and opened it. Then Ned stabbed the rear tire. The action brought him a strange satisfaction. He moved to the opposite side of the vehicle. He was now in between the van and Deputy Lockwood's truck. He punctured the Chevy's other rear tire. This action didn't bring as much joy as the first.

Ned then stabbed both tires on the driver's side of the deputy's truck. When he was at the front of the vehicle, he peered over the hood to check the fourth bungalow. All the curtains were closed.

Now, Grizzle and his crew were stuck at the Quik N Go. There was no escape for them until the marshals arrived. Ned moved toward the rear of the patrol truck.

No one had an option for freedom. A cruel smile spread on his lips. His joy quickly dissipated when he realized there was one more vehicle—Alden and Hattie's Navigator. Could Ned safely assume that Grizzle's crew disabled their SUV? Or should he go and verify it?

He knew what he needed to do, but he was cold, and his jeans were wet. He wanted the comfort of a bungalow and a set of new pants.

Comfort would have to wait if he wanted to ensure Grizzle didn't escape justice.

Ned Delahanty stooped his shoulders and pushed further into the night.

***

It only took a few minutes of hurrying for Ned to arrive at the last bungalow. The curtains were open in the windows, and the lights were on. Even though he couldn't hear what was occurring inside, Ned had a pretty good idea.

On the far side of the room, Alden and Hattie clung tightly to each other. They nervously looked on as Grizzle, Lockwood, and Ringo huddled together in conversation. Jumping on the two beds were the four girls. They smiled and laughed as they spun and kicked.

Ned swore to himself, "Kids."

With no one watching the windows, he hurried to the Lincoln Navigator. The entire time he moved, he kept an eye on the bungalow. When he neared the vehicle, he felt the tires, but his fingers were cold and stiff. He couldn't immediately tell if the tire was flat and the snow was too high for a visual inspection.

He stabbed the tire and was rewarded with a limp rubbery resistance. The tire was already disabled. Someone in Grizzle's crew had taken care of it.

But Ned needed to ensure that two tires were vandalized. No vehicle ever came with a second spare. He decided against creeping toward the front tire. That would put him dangerously close to the bungalow.

He shuffled around the rear of the large SUV to the other side, where he stabbed the second back tire. The knife sunk in solidly, and that sense of satisfaction returned.

The door to the bungalow opened. He stiffened.

"Those kids are giving me a migraine," Grizzle said.

"Can you imagine willingly doing that to yourself?" Ringo asked. "That's like hitting your thumb with a hammer then repeating it three more times just to make sure the first time hurt."

"Shh," Grizzle said.

"What do you see?" Lockwood asked.

"Shh," Grizzle angrily repeated.

Ned glanced around to see if an ambient light had created a shadow of himself. Not seeing any, he pressed harder into the back of the Navigator.

"Clerk," Grizzle said, "you don't know when to stop."

"How do you know it's the clerk?" Ringo asked.

Ned squatted lower and looked left and right. There was no way he'd given away his position.

Grizzle said, "Come out where we can see you."

"We promise not to shoot," Ringo added. "What? What'd I say?"

Ned wondered how Grizzle knew he was there.

"The snow around the vehicle is disturbed," Grizzle said. "It's only safe to assume you're the one who did so. Who else would be out in this weather? Poke your head out where we can see you. On my honor, I promise not to shoot."

"That's what I said," Ringo whined. "Why'd you get so mad at me for saying the same thing you did?"

Ned pulled the gun from his pocket. He peeked around the edge of the SUV and extended his gun.

Grizzle, Ringo, and Lockwood all pointed their guns at him.

The former marshal smiled grimly. "It seems you're at a disadvantage, clerk."

"Looks about right to me."

"How's that?"

Ned said, "The only one I'm interested in killing is you, Grizzle."

Ringo eyed the former marshal and took a step away to the left. Lockwood noticed her action and nonchalantly slid further to the right.

Grizzle muttered something under his breath that Ned couldn't hear. Both Lockwood and Ringo returned to their previous positions. The former marshal said, "But you're all out of bullets."

Ned squeezed the trigger, and the support

beam above the three splintered. Grizzle, Lockwood, and Ringo all flinched.

"Got five more," Ned said.

"It seems I have underestimated you."

"When was the last time you changed a tire?"

Grizzle cocked his head, then looked to Lockwood. "What's he talking about?"

The deputy shrugged.

Ned said, "I'd suggest you worry about that before you worry about me." He stayed behind the SUV as he backpedaled away. He wanted to keep the bungalow in sight.

"The van," Grizzle said.

"What about it?" Lockwood asked. "I didn't do anything to our vehicles."

"Check it out. *Now!*"

Ned continued to shuffle backward. When Grizzle appeared around the SUV, Ned shot in his direction. The former marshal dove into the snow. Ringo appeared around the other side of the Navigator, and she fired at Ned. He shot in her direction but purposefully missed. The bullet thunked into the SUV.

"Ah!" she screamed and plunged into the snowy roadway.

Ned backpedaled once more before spinning toward the Quik N Go.

As he ran along the building, he had only two thoughts.

First, he was down to three rounds. Second, how long would it be before the snow stopped and the marshals arrived?

Chapter 16

Ned clomped along the sidewalk and ran into the convenience store. He might have a minute, perhaps two, before Grizzle and his crew recovered their wits and followed him to the Quik N Go. Ned locked the door behind him.

Being out of the cold, blowing wind was an immediate welcome relief. His boots loudly squeaked as he hurried through the store. He slipped but caught himself on a shelf of packaged donuts. After righting himself, Ned grabbed a box and continued.

When he made it behind the counter, he dropped to his knees. Water from melting snow ran down his temples. He poked his head above the counter and searched for approaching crew members. When he didn't see anyone, he rested a second. Ned set his gun on the counter and opened the package. He shoved the first donut in his mouth and greedily ate.

Maybe Grizzle and the others weren't coming. Perhaps they'd gotten focused on the damaged tires of the van and the patrol car. It was likely that solving that problem had become the immediate concern. If that were the case, exacting revenge would be deemed secondary.

He swallowed and immediately shoved a second donut into his mouth.

What would Grizzle's plan be? If Ned were in the former marshal's shoes, what would he do?

Ned considered while he chomped on the donut. He decided he'd first try to find a suitable replacement tire from the other vehicles. He hadn't flattened all the tires on the van nor the deputy's truck, so only two were needed.

Ned hadn't bothered to check all the tires on the guest's vehicles. If Grizzle or his crew hadn't flattened them all, there might be a chance a couple would fit. They would have to consider only the tire size and the bolt configuration. Those were significant hurdles, but when a man's freedom rode on it, they were hurdles worth climbing over.

The longer he enjoyed the warmth of the convenience store and the sugary goodness of the donuts—he popped another into his mouth—the more convinced he became that the crew wasn't chasing him.

He removed his cell phone from his pocket and hit the redial button. The call was answered on the first ring.

"Horoscope Hook-up," a woman answered, "where we help you find the spirit of love."

Ned swallowed the last of his donut. "I need Amy at Psychic Outreach."

"Oh," the woman chuckled. "That's not how it works. You see, Psychic Outreach is a proactive marketing agency, and they only call out. They don't receive calls. I can understand your confusion and—"

"This is Beauregard Smith."

"Well, hello, Beauregard," the woman said in a lilted voice. "I'm Louise." He heard a keyboard clacking on the other end of the line. "I hope you're having a beautiful evening."

"Beau's my real name—"

"I see that.

"—and I'm in real trouble."

"You realize," Louise said in a lecturing tone, "that this call is a violation of our customer protocol."

"I don't have time to jump through bureaucratic hoops."

"Those hoops are put there for your safety and the safety of others."

"I understand but—"

"And did you know that you affect others by your daily choices?"

"Yeah, but—"

Louise continued. "This decision has impacted a lot more people than you think."

"Okay, but hear me out—"

"Did you even stop to think of others before acting in this manner?"

Ned closed his eyes and pinched the bridge of his nose. "Listen, lady—"

"Excuse me?"

He opened his eyes and took a deep, cleansing breath. "I'm in trouble."

"You called me 'lady.' That was rude and offensive."

"Is this call being recorded for training purposes?"

"Don't change the subject."

Ned's chin fell to his chest.

It sounded like Louise was tapping something

against a computer screen. "It says you're a Libra, but you're acting like an Aries."

Ned lifted his head above the counter. He searched for anyone approaching. "You're complaining about my tone?"

"That's right," Louise said. "You're aggressive, and I feel intimidated."

"We're on a phone."

"So? People can be intimidated on a telephone."

Ned grabbed the gun from the counter. "I've been shot at, and you're complaining about feelings?"

"False equivalencies are the types of things I'm talking about."

"Lady—"

Louise shouted, "See!"

"Armed gunmen have taken over the Quik N Go in Eagle's Feet, Wyoming."

"That doesn't give you the right to behave in this manner."

Ned lowered the phone and stared at it. When he returned it to his ear, she was still talking, "—and for your information, this call *is* being recorded. I am hopeful others can learn from my emotional trauma and avoid—."

Ned interrupted. "Can I speak to your supervisor?"

"Why?" Louise asked suspiciously. "What did I do?"

"I need help."

"Yes, you do." More keyboard clicking. "There are plenty of excellent books on anger management and gender relationships that I can recommend."

"No. I'd like to talk about the gunmen who've taken over the convenience store."

Louise stopped clacking her keyboard. "This isn't a joke."

"I know that."

"Gunmen don't take over a convenience store. Who has ever heard of such a thing?"

"I've disarmed a couple of them, but the group's leader is a former marshal named Grizzle."

Louise stopped typing. "Titus Grizzle?"

"That's right. And he's—"

"Titus Grizzle is there now?"

"That's what I said, so if you'd let me speak to a supervisor—"

"Hold please."

The line went silent.

Ned shoved another donut into his mouth and ate. This one didn't taste as wonderful as the first.

***

After Ned finished speaking with a Horoscope Hotline supervisor, he flipped the phone closed and tucked it into his pocket. He crumbled the donuts' packaging and threw it into the corner. He stared at the ball of trash for a moment, then stood. Ned picked it up and tossed it into the garbage can at the end of the counter.

He was now sure that Grizzle and his

remaining crew were figuring out how to secure replacement tires. They hadn't approached him while he conversed with the hotline's supervisor. Even if the crew had taken their time getting to him, they would have arrived by now.

Assuming that Grizzle's crew could get tires from another rig to fit on their van, what would be their next course of action? Ned imagined that they would head out in the snowstorm.

But if they couldn't do that, what would the crew do? Would they wait until the storm broke? What choice would they have? That created a problem.

No, that wasn't true.

The problem already existed—Ned had exacerbated it.

The marshals were mustering forces to rescue Ned. They had started before this latest call. However, travel to the Quik N Go was hampered by the blizzard. Not even a local cop could get to them.

So, if Grizzle's crew waited for the storm to break, they might find themselves confronted by all that arriving law enforcement. The former marshal would grab the civilians staying in the bungalows and hold them until he negotiated some sort of safe passage. Ned explained his thoughts to the hotline supervisor but was rewarded with, "We'll take it under advisement."

Ned didn't want any harm to come to the guests in the bungalows. Therefore, he needed to create additional problems to keep Grizzle and his crew occupied.

He walked to the back of the store and flicked several switches. The gas station came alive. Even through the falling snow, Ned could see the pylon sign flicker several times before glowing. That meant the lower sign with the rearranged letters—*Help! Robbers!*—might be visible in the unlikely event someone passed by.

The lights on the canopied fuel island also fluttered to life. It was an illuminated oasis in the middle of the blizzard.

Ned turned on the radio and turned the station back to 106.9 FM. Some poppy metal song about "Cherry Pie" played through the cheap speakers. He turned it up.

He tucked his gun into his pocket and then walked to the restroom. Using a key in his pocket, he unlocked the door.

Paul lay on his back with his legs secured to the railing on the wall. His hands were still tied behind his back.

"Doing okay?" Ned asked.

"Mmffph," Paul said into the duct tape covering his mouth.

He thumbed back into the main part of the store. "I put on some music for you."

"Mmffph mfmphyl mmfphyll."

"It was no problem. My pleasure. Is it loud enough?"

"Mmffph mpmfphyl mmffphly."

"All right," Ned said. "You take it easy. And don't forget, the toilet is broken."

Ned closed the bathroom door. As he headed

for the exit, Ned stopped and grabbed one of the orange beanies. He swore he'd never wear one of them or the trucker hats, but now was not the time to worry about how cool he looked. He pulled the beanie on, tugging it down over his ears.

Outside the store, he took a moment to lock the door. If Grizzle wanted to save Paul, he was going to make it hard on the man. Grizzle might want to enter the store by breaking the glass, but it would take far more effort than he realized.

Ned moved toward the end of the building. He peered around the corner to make sure no one was coming. He stepped into the deep snow and headed around back.

***

Ned hesitated at the rear of the Quik N Go. He saw the shape of the first bungalow, but that was it. The heavy snowfall and the poor lighting made it nearly impossible to see further back. If he couldn't see any of the crew, he figured it worked in the opposite direction as well.

He hurried as quickly as he could across the roadway. His boot caught in something, and he fell.

"You hear that?" Lockwood said.

"Hear what?" Grizzle asked.

"I swore I heard something."

Ned didn't know where the two men were, so he low-crawled as quickly as he could through the snow. He moved toward his pickup, which was parked out front of the first bungalow.

"This is a Land Rover," Grizzle said.

Ned froze. He pressed himself deeper into the snow, but he couldn't see under the truck. It was too deep.

"So?" Lockwood said. "Maybe it'll work. Let's take it."

"It won't work," Grizzle said. "And I'm not standing out in this cold any longer than I have to."

Ned pulled the gun from his pocket and brought himself to his knees. Wetness soaked his jeans, and he was freezing. The revolver in his hands felt like a chunk of ice.

"Why don't you call dispatch for help?" Grizzle asked.

"And tell them what? That I'm back on duty and out of my jurisdiction?"

"Tell them you got caught in the storm."

Lockwood laughed. "You got an answer for everything."

Ned didn't dare peer through a window at the two men. If they saw him, he'd have a problem. It was two against one, and he only had three rounds left in the gun. To make matters worse, he felt sluggish. The cold was getting to him. He needed a change of clothes.

"What about your truck?" Grizzle said.

"I got the same problem as you—only one spare."

"But it's got the lights and sirens. Let's work on fixing that."

"We can't fit everyone into my truck," Lockwood said.

"Forget them. Focus on you and me."

"Is that why you're not worried about finding the others?"

"Listen," Grizzle said. "They got caught. We'll fix your truck, move the money, and leave them holding the bag." The former marshal's voice faded into the distance.

Ned rose slightly to look over the back window. It was hard to see, but two shadowy figures moved further away.

He stood and hurried toward the first bungalow.

Chapter 17

Five of them eyed Ned as he set the revolver on top of the dresser.

Brick and Kiki huddled together. In her arms, she cradled Travis the cat who seemed to be enjoying her attention. He nuzzled his head into Kiki's hand. Donovan and Sophia sat on the edge of the bed. John stood near the bathroom with frequent glances into the smaller room.

Ned also set his cell phone and keys on top of the dresser. He turned to the group and unzipped his wet coat. The garment slipped from his shoulders, and he let it fall to the floor. A wet long-sleeved shirt clung to his chest.

"You look like a drowned rat," Brick said.

Kiki straightened and smiled appreciatively. "I wouldn't go that far."

Sophia murmured something in support of Kiki's assessment.

Donovan scowled at his girlfriend as he motioned to Ned's beanie. "What about that hat? It makes him look like a pencil eraser."

"I don't know." Sophia's eyes flicked to the logo on the orange beanie. "I'd rather like to know what he got at the Quik N Go."

It was Kiki's turn to mutter her support.

Brick smirked. "Probably dysentery."

Kiki rolled her eyes before leaning down to the cat in her arms. She spoke softly, but the room was so small everyone could hear. "Cheddar Sprocket thinks somebody's jealous," she cooed in baby talk.

"It's Travis," Ned said. He tugged the orange beanie from his head and tossed it on top of the coat.

"And I'm not jealous," Brick added. "I'm just saying that the Quik N Go probably isn't the cleanest place in the world."

Kiki waved one of the cat's paws. "Who's gonna be a star?"

Ned ran his fingers through his wet hair, then he knelt and yanked up a pant leg. He pulled the knife from the boot and tossed it with a clatter upon the dresser. When Ned began untying his boot, he paused long enough to eye John. "Where's your friend?"

He frowned. "I'd hardly call us friends."

There was a muffled protest from the bathroom.

"Regardless," Ned said, "how is he?"

"He's upright."

"Bring him out. We need to talk."

John disappeared into the bathroom.

"Why'd you put him in there?" Ned asked Donovan.

"Looking at him made me feel bad."

Sophia nodded. "Yeah. He made us think he was nice."

Ned finished untying the boot, stood, and kicked it from his foot. He knelt again and started on the other.

John pulled George by his armpits out of the

restroom. George's hands and feet remained bound, and the heels of his shoes dragged along the carpet. The strip of duct tape still covered George's mouth.

Ned yanked the laces loose on his second boot. "Let him speak."

John bent over, grabbed a corner of the duct tape between two fingers, and ripped the strip from George's lips. The man yowled with pain.

"You need to make a decision," Ned said.

George narrowed his eyes. "What's this decision?"

Ned stood and kicked the second boot free. "The marshals are on the way."

"So?"

"And they know about Grizzle."

"How?" George looked at John. "Did you tell him?"

John motioned to Ned. "Listen to the man."

"They're putting together a force right now. I'm not sure how quickly they can get to us, but they're coming. Trust me."

"That means they know about us?" George asked. He looked sorrowfully at John. "We're done for."

Ned moved toward a dresser. "All they know is your nickname." He yanked open a drawer and pulled out a black t-shirt. "Both John and I have called the hotline and told them about Grizzle."

"You're in the program?" George asked.

"I think that's why you guys came here," Ned said. "Grizzle was looking for Kenny Piersee, but he died."

Ned tugged the wet shirt over his head. The fireball tattoo on his right hand turned into a snake that wrapped around his arm and ended near his neck. A menagerie of images covered his other arm, his chest, and his back.

Kiki grinned appreciatively. "Nice ink."

"I've never liked tattoos," Sophia murmured, "but I think I'm changing my mind."

Brick coughed loudly, and Donovan grumbled something about being born with the right genetics. Both men stepped between their girlfriends and Ned. The women tried to see around their boyfriends. It was like a strange dance with no music.

"So, what?" George said. "You think we're gonna have a chance to claim our innocence after all the places we robbed?"

Ned shrugged. "It depends. Grizzle threatened you. You should call in and tell your story like John did." He grabbed a black t-shirt and slipped it on.

Kiki and Sophia groaned with disappointment.

"Grizzle and Lockwood are going to abandon you all," Ned said. He reached into another drawer and pulled out a pair of jeans. He tossed them on top of the dresser. "I overheard that when I was outside."

"Overheard how?" George lifted his secured wrists in protest.

"Give the man a chance," John said.

Ned continued. "Grizzle and the deputy are

preoccupied with finding a way out of here." He unbuttoned his jeans.

"Hey, bud!" Donovan said.

All eyes turned his way.

Donovan motioned toward Ned's hands. "Would you mind? There are ladies present."

Ned looked at Kiki and Sophia. "I apologize." He rebuttoned his jeans.

"It's totally fine," Kiki said. "Don't mind me. Go right ahead."

"Don't stop on my account," Sophia added. "I'm not offended in any way."

Kiki waved the cat's paw. "And Cheddar Sprocket is good with it, too. Yes, changing out here is totally cat-approved." Kiki looked up with a wide grin.

Brick angrily cleared his throat and thumbed toward the restroom. "Take it on the road, pervert."

Ned grabbed the jeans from the top of the dresser and padded toward the bathroom. Once there, he quickly peeled off the wet pants and threw them into the bathtub. He put on the dry jeans and exited the small room.

John was now at the front window. "The store's lights are back on."

"I did that," Ned said. "To give Grizzle one more thing to worry about."

John let the curtain fall back into place. "You think he'll spend time shutting them off?"

Ned shrugged. "Maybe he'll waste time trying to get into the store. If not, maybe somebody shows up and sees the note I left asking for help.”

“What if he’s got more guys meeting him?” Brick asked. “Won’t those lights just be a beacon for them?”

“Yeah,” Donavon added. “What if you just helped the bad guys? That’s a good question.”

Kiki shook her head and spoke to the cat in the baby voice again. “We definitely think somebody’s jealous.”

“I’m not jealous,” Brick and Donovan said in unison. Realizing they spoke together, they motioned at each other and said in unison once more, “We’re not jealous.”

Ned studied John, then shifted his gaze to George. “Did Grizzle say anything about more guys?”

George rolled his lower lip down while he thought. “I don’t think so. He said he was meeting someone so that must have been the deputy, right?”

“Why didn’t he give Lockwood a nickname like the rest of you?” Ned asked.

“I think,” John said as he moved across the room to stand near George, “he knew Lockwood was coming in uniform. There must have been a reason he wanted a patrol car.”

Ned studied both John and George. “Well?”

“Yeah,” Sophia said. “Don’t leave us in the dark.”

Kiki whispered to the cat, “We really should have this on camera, Cheddar Sprocket. Such good content lost.”

She lifted the cat so it could look her in the

eye. "Yeah, Kiki," she said in a squeaky feline voice, "Too bad that mean man broke your cell phones."

John frowned, then turned back to Ned. "You've got to understand this about Grizzle. He didn't tell us anything about the jobs until right before we did them. He might have planned them out, but we didn't know anything until the jump-off. When I first got brought on, it was just Grizzle, Paul, and me. Those were smaller jobs that we could handle. Then we picked up George, and the jobs got a little more complicated. When we added Ringo is when the bank heists started."

Ned cocked his head. "So, you think Lockwood's arrival means the crew was about to do something bigger?"

"Stands to reason," John said. "And if he wanted Lockwood's uniform and patrol car, that meant one of two things."

George held his bound hands in the air. "That he needed them to gain entrance for a bigger heist."

John shrugged. "Or he needed them to help with the getaway."

Ned rubbed his chin. "But now that plan has been scrapped or at least delayed due to the blizzard and the manhunt."

"So, what are you thinking?" George said. "That we make a stand?" He motioned toward the dresser with his bound hands. "Using one gun and a pocketknife? This ain't *The Magnificent Seven*."

Brick counted the people in the room. "We've got seven people."

Kiki baby-talked to the cat. "And my followers think I'm pretty magnificent."

"I'm sure they do," Sophia muttered with a little too much venom.

"Wait a minute," Donovan interjected. "We're going to do what now? Make a stand?"

"How many rounds are in that gun?" John asked.

"Three," Ned said.

Donovan looked to Brick. "Are you hearing this? We're supposed to make a stand with three bullets?"

Brick held up his hand to stop Donovan from talking further. "What if we just take off? Take our chances with the storm?"

Ned shook his head. "Your vehicles all have flat tires. Grizzle made sure you couldn't escape."

"He touched my truck?" Brick asked.

"Ours, too?" Donovan asked.

"Gimme that gun," Brick said. "I'll take care of this myself." He reached for the gun but didn't move closer to the dresser to get it.

Sophia picked up the gun and offered it to Brick. He glanced at Ned and chuckled nervously. "It's probably better that you have it."

Ned took the gun from Sophia and tucked it into his jeans. "There's not a vehicle on this property that doesn't have at least two flat tires."

George's brow furrowed. "That means you

flattened our van and the deputy's truck, too?"

"*Their* van," John corrected.

"Why'd you do that?" George asked. "Why would you want to keep them here?"

"Because I didn't know what Grizzle would do with them before he left." Ned motioned toward the two couples. "Would he let them live or since they'd seen him…" He let his question trail off.

Donovan threw his hands in the air. "You think he'd kill us? I don't want to die."

Sophia rolled her eyes.

"We didn't do anything," Donovan said. He pleaded with Ned. "Maybe you should talk with them, bud. You know, negotiate something."

"There's nothing to negotiate," Ned said. "They're stuck here with us. Now, it's time for a new plan."

"What plan?" Sophia asked. She moved next to Donovan, but she eyed Ned differently than before.

Kiki moved closer too. "Whatever the plan, we'll help." She cast a glance at Sophia. "Even Cheddar Sprocket will help."

Brick ruefully shook his head. "What's this big plan of yours?"

The two couples surrounded Ned, and he felt closed in. "Excuse me," he said and stepped past Brick. He picked up his boots and sat on the edge of the bed. "We stay in this room and wait for them—"

"Works for me," Donovan said.

"Me, too," Brick said. "Especially since my truck isn't going anywhere."

Ned frowned. "We stay in this room and wait for them to attack us?"

"Oh," Donovan said, "that probably doesn't work."

Brick shook his head. "Waiting probably isn't a good idea."

Ned shoved his foot into a boot. "That's why I think we should take the fight to them."

Donovan lifted his hands into the air. "Hold on there, Rambo."

Brick pointed at Donovan. "Yeah, slow up, Terminator."

Ned shoved a foot into the second boot. "What's the problem?"

"There's got to be some middle ground," Donovan said, "between waiting to be attacked or attacking them."

"There's not."

Donovan put his hands on his hips. "That doesn't make any sense. We could run. That's an option, and that's in the middle ground."

John said, "He just told you that none of the vehicles have all their tires."

Donovan's head bounced from side to side. "But we could drive for a little bit and get away from here."

"Then freeze to death," George offered. "You don't seem to think very far out."

Ned laced up the first boot. "You don't have to do anything."

"But you're taking the gun," Donovan said.

"That's right."

Donovan eyed the sole gun remaining on the

dresser. He grabbed it and held it without confidence. "I'll hold on to this."

"You do that." Ned laced his second boot. "Just so you know, they always shoot the guy with the gun first."

Donovan's eyes widened. He offered the gun to Brick, who shook his head.

Sophia hissed, "Put it back."

John took the gun from Donovan. "So what's the plan?"

Ned finished changing by dropping the pant leg over his boot. "There's a family in bungalow five. It's time we got them out." He grabbed the knife from the dresser and moved to George. "Are you with us or against us?"

George extended his wrists.

"That's not an answer."

"I'll help." He looked at John. "He and I didn't want to be a part of this mess to begin with."

Ned cut the duct tape around George's wrists. He looked at Kiki. "Would you mind bringing Travis?"

"Cheddar Sprocket," she corrected.

"I don't want to leave him alone."

Kiki leaned down to the cat that she still held in her arms. "Isn't this exciting?" Her voice rang with the baby talk. "We're going on an adventure!"

Chapter 18

They marched single file through the storm. Whistling gusts of wind propelled the snow sideways. The accumulation on the ground was far more than two feet now.

A man said something behind Ned that sounded like complaining. He couldn't be sure, but he suspected it was Donovan. Ned glanced back, but everyone trudged forward with their heads down to ward off the chilly wind.

Puffs of white danced across the ground.

Ned paused at the front of the Quik N Go and peeked around the corner. Seeing no one, he hurried to the door and unlocked it. He entered the store to another infuriatingly happy metal song.

He stomped his feet on the mat as the others passed him into the store. When John entered, Ned shut the door.

"Paul's in the restroom." Ned motioned down the hallway.

Donovan's face darkened. "You told me it was out of order."

"He's tied up."

"Right." Donovan chuckled and glanced at Sophia. "I knew that."

Her smile was meant to placate. "Of course you did."

Kiki opened her coat, and the cat jumped

from her arms to the floor. "We made it, Sprocket."

"What happened to the Cheddar?" Brick asked.

"He likes it better because it's cooler." She watched the cat with odd appreciation. "He's the best boy."

Brick stared at her.

"I'm hungry," she said and wandered off. Brick dutifully followed.

Sophia and Donovan tagged along in search of food.

Ned faced John and George. "I'm going after that other family."

"We'll come along," John said.

"We?" George asked.

"Someone should stay here." Ned glanced at the two couples standing in front of a cooler door. They found a couple of Hot Pockets and compared the caloric impact of each. "They aren't prepared to stand up to Grizzle."

"Neither am I," said George. A sudden sheepishness crossed his face. "If I'm being honest."

Ned considered the man, then eyed John. "You both should stay here."

John nodded. "I'll watch out for them."

"Lock the door behind me," Ned said.

"It's glass," George said. "If they want in, they're getting in."

"Trust me," Ned said. "It'll hold." He slipped into the night. Behind him, the lock clicked as it dropped into place.

Ned trotted around the corner and then along the side of the building until he neared the corner. He carried the gun with both hands. He slowed and peered out to the nearest bungalow—the fifth. It was hard to see, but clearly, two people stood outside the structure.

Ned crouched and hurried forward. As he neared the Lincoln Navigator, he slowed further. Slowly, he peeked around the edge of the vehicle.

Alden Fodey and Ringo stood on the small porch and smoked cigarettes. The interior of the bungalow could be seen through the windows. The four girls bounced up and down on the beds. Hattie stood nearby with her arms crossed and a sour expression on her face.

"I don't know how you do it," Ringo said.

Alden inhaled on his cigarette. "It's a gift."

"But four kids?"

"It's only incrementally harder after the second."

"Incrementally?"

Alden waved his cigarette around. "It's like you're swimming, and someone hands you a concrete block. You might be able to keep swimming with that first block, but if someone hands you a second? You're done."

"So the third and fourth block—"

"Are like the third and fourth kids." Alden inhaled again on his cigarette. "You don't sink any faster."

Some angry cursing could be heard in the direction of the other bungalows.

"What's got them so steamed?" Alden asked.

Ringo shrugged. "My boss and his friend aren't car guys."

"Maybe if they hadn't flattened everyone's tires, then this problem could have been avoided."

"They didn't flatten their own."

"The clerk did that? He seemed like a nice guy."

"Isn't that how it goes?" She inhaled on her cigarette. "It's always the nice ones who fool you. That's why I like bad men. They're rotten inside, but they'll never let me down."

Ned stepped around the back of the SUV. As he went, he straightened and pointed his gun at Ringo. "Keep your hands where I can see them."

She was inhaling when he spoke. Ringo left the cigarette in her mouth as both hands went skyward.

"Hey," Alden said, "it's you. Where'd you get the gun?"

"I took it from one of her friends." Ned moved forward and eyed Ringo. "Where's yours?"

With a single finger, she pointed down toward her waist.

"Don't do anything stupid," Ned said.

Ringo bit the end of the cigarette. Through clenched teeth, she said, "I wouldn't think of it."

Ned reached under her jacket and removed her gun.

"Not that it matters," Alden said, "but she hasn't shown the gun to the girls."

"You're right," Ned said.

He smiled. "I am?"

"It doesn't matter. Go inside and get the girls ready."

"For what?"

"We're moving everyone to the convenience store."

Alden knocked some ash from his cigarette. "Why would we do that? We've got beds in here and—"

"Her boss is going to use your family as hostages when the marshals show up."

"Marshals?" Alden said.

Ned eyed Ringo. "She didn't tell you? They're on the way." He thumbed toward the convenience store.

"But it doesn't make sense for us to go up there," Alden said.

"Trust me."

Alden's eyes dropped. "I don't want this to sound bad, but—"

Ned pointed the gun at him. "Does it make you feel better if I force you to do it?"

"Strangely, yes."

Inside the bungalow, the girls screamed and laughed.

Alden paused to consider his cigarette. "You know, I'm only about half done with this. What do you say if we enjoy a couple more minutes out here so I can finish?"

"I'll tell you what," Ned said. "I'll take Ringo back to the store, and you take your chances with her boss."

Alden's eyes narrowed. "It's becoming

increasingly obvious that you don't have kids." He dropped the cigarette and crushed it out with his toe. "I'll be back."

When the front door shut behind Alden, a cheer erupted inside the bungalow.

Ringo whispered, "We can go now."

"We're waiting."

She glanced through the window. "Yeah, but the kids."

"I hear you," Ned said, "but we're waiting."

They both turned to watch the chaos inside the bungalow. Alden and Hattie herded the girls toward their coats. The children jumped across the beds and shouted with laughter.

Ned frowned.

***

When the Fodeys stepped outside, Ned moved off the small porch. Ringo flicked her cigarette away. It was her third since Alden went inside.

Hattie turned to her daughters and bent low. "Remember, girls. No talking." She put a finger to her lips. "Shhh."

The children nodded solemnly.

Alden pulled the door closed. "We're ready."

"Let's go," Ned whispered. He motioned toward Ringo. "Lead the way."

She trudged ahead with her head bowed against the blowing snow. Ringo shoved her hands into her pockets to protect them from the cold.

The group spread out as they crossed the

back road. Ringo led with Ned close behind her. After them, the four children waddled through the snow and were followed by their parents.

Ringo slipped and fell. With her hands in her pockets, she had no way to stop her fall. Ned reached for her but froze when the girls squealed. This was followed by the unrestrained laughter of children who had just witnessed an adult's unexpected pratfall.

"Girls," Hattie whispered.

"What's that!" Grizzle yelled from the darkness.

"Jail break!" Lockwood shouted.

Ned shoved the gun into the front of his pants. Then he grabbed the two nearest girls and slung them around his waist. "Go," he said to Alden and Hattie. Each of them held a child and ran toward the building.

"Get going," Ned said to Ringo.

She'd pushed herself up to her hands and feet. "I'm not going anywhere."

"Get back here!" Grizzle yelled. He sounded closer.

Ned kicked Ringo hard in the rear. "Move!"

She popped up to her feet and hurried toward the building.

As Ned ran, the children bounced on his hips. This caused an awkward gait. The girls he carried laughed with each jounce. One of them even cried, "Whee!" and stuck her arms out in front as if she was flying.

"Clerk!" Grizzle shouted. "I see you!"

Up ahead, Ringo rounded the corner. Ned was

close behind.

A gun fired. A second shot went off.

As Ned stepped onto the front sidewalk, Alden and Hattie were just entering the store. After Ringo entered, Ned moved sideways through the door. He set the two girls down, and they rejoined their sisters. The four of them ran up and down the aisles with their arms extended.

John shut the door and spun the lock. Ned handed him Ringo's gun.

Titus Grizzle and Deputy Lockwood tromped along the sidewalk. When they made it to the front door, Grizzle angrily yanked on the handle.

"Let us in!" the former marshal hollered.

Ned waved them along. "We're closed."

Grizzle's eyes widened. "John! I see you. Open this door." He yanked on the handle, and the door rattled loudly.

John moved next to Ned.

"That's how it's gonna be?" Grizzle shouted. He pointed at John. "Remember this when the mob comes for you!" His eyes scanned the interior of the store. "George! George! Let us in."

The boring man lifted a bag of potato chips and pretended to study their contents.

"You're done for, too, George." Grizzle's face pinched with anger. "When they find you, I hope you remember this moment."

The children screamed with excitement as they continued their flight through the store.

"Girls," Hattie said. "Not now."

But they didn't listen.

Grizzle pounded on the door. "Ringo! Get over

here and let us in."

She made a move toward the door, but John cut her off. "Not a good idea."

Her gaze fell to the gun he held. She looked over John's shoulder to Grizzle. "He says no."

Lockwood tapped Grizzle's arm and said something to the man. Grizzle listened, then turned back to the door. He banged on the glass. "If you don't open, we're gonna shoot our way in."

Ned said to John, "Get everyone away from the windows." Then he eyed the group. "Get in the storeroom."

Alden and Hattie herded the girls toward the storage room. Donovan and Sophia followed them in.

Brick pulled Kiki reluctantly toward the back of the store. "Let's get out of the way."

She frowned as she stroked the cat. "Think how cool this would have been had we filmed it. It would have totally gone viral."

Brick tugged on her once more, and they disappeared into the storeroom.

Now, it was just Ned and three members of Grizzle's crew—John, George, and Ringo.

"Last chance!" Grizzle shouted. "Or we start blasting."

"Give him what he wants," Ringo said. "I promise he'll leave them alone." She motioned toward the storeroom.

"The marshals aren't going to make it in time," John added.

George headed toward the cashier's counter.

"We should probably take cover before the bullets start flying."

Ringo moved toward the hallway with the restroom. "I'm not scared." She backpedaled as she talked. "I'm only doing this out of an abundance of caution. You know, in case of flying glass, or exploding sodas, or things that can get in my eyes."

John waved her on, then studied Ned. "Are you just going to stand here?"

"What's wrong with it?" Ned asked.

"We're in the middle of the store."

"I've got faith."

"Then why get everyone into the storeroom?"

Ned eyed him. "I didn't want them to see my faith."

John glanced at Ringo and then George. "Maybe I'll stand with you."

"You don't have to."

"Yeah, I do," said John. "I'm tired of hiding." He moved closer to Ned.

Outside, Grizzle and Lockwood stepped back several paces. They lifted their guns.

John squinted and turned his face away. Ned, however, stared on defiantly.

Grizzle scowled before firing. Lockwood immediately joined in. Flames shot out of both of their guns. Bullets repeatedly hit the front window with deafening thuds. From inside the storeroom, someone screamed—it sounded like Donovan.

John flinched several times as the rounds impacted against the windows. Slowly, recognition set in, and he cast a disbelieving glance at Ned. "Bulletproof glass?"

That realization must have also occurred to Grizzle and Lockwood because they stopped shooting. Both men dashed forward to inspect the minor damage caused to the windows.

Grizzle's gaze shifted to Ned. He angrily banged against the window. "Get out here!"

Lockwood even kicked the door several times to no effect.

Ned waved.

A pair of headlights pierced the darkness from the west. A loud rumbling soon followed. Grizzle and Lockwood spun to face the newcomer.

The vehicle bounced into the parking lot. As it drew closer to the gas pumps, its shape could be made out. It wasn't a car or a truck but rather a military-style tracked vehicle. It had two articulated sections and was painted camouflage green.

Grizzle and Lockwood raised their guns and fired a couple of shots. However, neither man had bothered to reload and were quickly out of rounds.

The vehicle swung wide and jerked to a stop. It rocked back and forth as shadows spilled from the far side of the transport. Soon police officers in different colored uniforms peered around the edge of the tracked vehicle. They clutched pistols in their hands.

One of them yelled, "Drop your weapons and get on the ground!"

Grizzle and Lockwood ran in opposite directions around the back of the building.

Eight officers flanked out from both sides of the camouflaged vehicle. They lined up in four-person lines and trotted after the former marshal and the wayward deputy.

An older white man stepped around the front of the vehicle. He wore a camouflaged winter coat and a black beret. On both sides of him were two young soldiers dressed similarly. Their M16 rifles were raised at the ready.

The man walked with his shoulders pulled back, and his head held high. He clutched an automatic pistol in his right hand. When he made it to the front door, the man pulled on the handle and rattled the door against its lock. He made eye contact with Ned and then stepped back.

Ned unlocked the door and opened it. The man entered the room and surveyed the others. When his gaze returned to Ned, the man nodded. "I'm Captain Tester with the 297th Infantry Regiment. Did someone call for help?"

"I did."

Tester studied him. "I'm not sure who you know, son, but they called the governor who rousted my general. The ball rolled downhill until it landed with me. I was told we had twenty minutes to get our transport rolling. I said there was no way we could get it staffed with men, but the governor assured me there were law enforcement officers standing by the armory."

Ringo and George came out from their hiding

places.

"Is it just you four?" the captain asked.

"There's a group of civilians in the storeroom," Ned said. "And one tied up in the restroom."

Tester raised an eyebrow.

"A bad guy," Ned clarified.

The captain grunted. "We were told there were five suspects."

Ned considered lying. He didn't want to rat out John. Heck, he didn't want to snitch on George or Ringo, either. Ned paused to consider the proper words. When he opened his mouth to speak, John set his hand on Ned's shoulder.

"We were part of it."

Captain Tester eyed John and Ned. "You two?"

"Not this guy." John patted Ned's shoulder. "Us three." He jerked his head toward Ringo and George.

Ringo rolled her eyes. "You talk too much, John. You know that?"

Tester motioned his two soldiers forward. "Watch those three." His gaze slid to Ned. "And what about you? How are you involved?"

Ned motioned toward the counter. "I'm nobody," he said. "I'm just the clerk."

Chapter 19

A squeal of little girl laughter came from inside the storeroom.

Captain Tester said, "Sounds like they're having a good time. Let them out."

"Shouldn't we wait?" Ned asked. "At least until Grizzle and Lockwood are apprehended."

"If you like," the captain said and crossed his arms.

Several officers marched Lockwood up the sidewalk from the west end of the building. His hands were cuffed behind his back.

The same scene played out on the east end. Grizzle shuffled with his head down and his hands behind his back.

"Well, look at that," Tester said. He stepped to the door and pulled it open. The ten men—eight officers of the law and their quarry—walked in.

"Any trouble?" the captain asked.

"This one tried to convince me that he's a former marshal." An officer lifted his chin toward Ned and John. "And that he's been chasing a crew across several states."

Ned pointed at Grizzle. "He was the mastermind of the whole thing."

The captain squinted. "That's a liberal use of the term."

"The clerk's right," John said. "He forced us

to commit those crimes.”

Tester unfolded his arms. “We’ll let these officers figure that out.”

The cops separated Grizzle and Lockwood by moving them to opposite sides of the store.

“Now,” the captain said, “about those people waiting in the storeroom.”

When Ned opened the door, the Fodey girls burst free like a can of shaken soda.

“Girls!” Hattie cried from the storeroom, but her plea went unheeded.

The children ran by Ned and the captain without any concern. Their shrieks and giggles filled the air. The girls sprinted through the Quik N Go tapping everything within reach.

Hattie was the next out, and she paused long enough to take in the scene of Captain Tester and his two soldiers. Her second cry of “Girls!” went ignored just like the first. She scampered after the smallest of the marauders.

Alden Fodey stepped out and acknowledged the captain with a nod. His gaze quickly passed over the assembled police officers and the handcuffed men.

Three of the Fodey girls twirled past with their arms extended wide. It was as if they were tops spinning across a kitchen table. The youngest child was cornered near the coolers by Mrs. Fodey. The little one had been abandoned by her siblings and no longer screeched.

“All seems normal,” Alden said.

Captain Tester watched the commotion in the corner. “Your wife could use some help.”

"She's got it under control." He patted his coat pocket. "There's something I need to do outside."

Kiki wandered out of the storeroom with Travis in her arms. She gently stroked the purring tom's fur as she watched the three girls bustle about the Quik N Go. "I want one."

Brick moved next to her. "A cat?"

When the girls shrieked with laughter, Kiki's eyes softened. "They're delightful."

"But what about your channel?"

"We'll make a new one."

Ned asked the captain, "Can they go back to their bungalows?"

Tester nodded. "Yes. One of the officers will be by to get their statements."

Kiki handed the cat to Ned and then made for the exit with Brick. The two young soldiers leaned together and whispered as the couple walked by. No words were exchanged before Kiki and Brick pushed open the door and left the Quik N Go.

Ned stuck his head into the storeroom. Donovan and Sophia stood together in an embrace.

"It's over," Ned said. "You can come out."

"That was horrible," Donovan muttered.

"The worst," Sophia agreed.

"Everything is safe," Ned said. "Grizzle and Lockwood are no longer a threat."

"Grizzle?" Donovan's face pinched.

Sophia pulled back. "Lockwood?"

Donovan pointed. "We're talking about

those—" His face contorted as he struggled to find a word worthy enough for the moment.

Now, Sophia pointed. "Those—" she said but stopped as she also couldn't find a description strong enough for her emotions.

Ned violated his no-swearing rule by uttering, "Kids?"

Both Donovan and Sophia shuddered.

"We are *never* having one," Sophia said.

Donovan took her face in his hands. "I've never loved you more than in this moment."

When they kissed, Ned shut the storeroom door. His phone buzzed, and he pulled it from his pocket.

***

The snow stopped as daylight broke. Large trucks plowed the highway. They sent plumes of powder to the sides of the roadway.

"Won't be long," John said, tapping his Styrofoam cup against Ned's.

They had spent the night in the convenience store with Captain Tester, his soldiers, and the assembled group of officers from the Wyoming State Patrol, the Natrona County Sheriff's Office, and the Casper Police Department.

The law enforcement officers had volunteered to travel with the National Guard members. It reminded Ned of the old westerns he watched with his grandmother where a hastily formed posse tracked down some evil men.

Seated in the far corner were Titus Grizzle

and Deputy Lockwood. Their hands remained cuffed behind their backs. Next to them, Paul sat sullenly. The duct tape had been removed from his hands and feet. Handcuffs now dangled from his wrists.

Several feet away, George and Ringo shared a box of donuts.

The cops clustered together and chatted with Captain Tester. The two young soldiers stood near Grizzle, Lockwood, and Paul. The soldiers played with their cell phones instead of actively guarding the arrested men.

Meanwhile, Ned and John leaned against the cashier's counter and sipped coffee.

"What're they like?" John asked.

"Who?"

"Your inspector."

Ned shrugged. "She's all right."

"Got a woman, huh?" John nodded with some appreciation. "I bet that's great. Probably more understanding of your feelings and such."

"Yeah."

The dark-haired soldier looked up from his phone. His face brightened. "I told you."

The other soldier leaned over to his friend so they could watch the small screen together.

"Grizzle was a terrible inspector," John said. "He never cared anything about how it felt to be living a lie. His replacement was better, but he never asked how I felt about being in the program. You think your lady marshal would ever do what Grizzle did?"

Ned shook his head. "The worst she's ever

done is named me Skeeter."

John studied him from the corner of his eye. "You've had more identities than this one?"

"Haven't you?"

"This is my only one, and I've had it for more than a decade."

Ned grunted.

"If you've had more than one," John said, "you're probably doing something wrong."

"They haven't been my fault."

John looked at him dubiously.

Ned frowned. "They haven't *all* been my fault."

"My grandmother used to tell me that I was the common denominator in all my problems. I never believed her until after I was arrested."

Before Ned could argue, the dark-haired soldier looked at him and said, "Dude!" Everyone in the store fell silent and turned the soldier's way. He lifted his phone and moved toward Ned. "I *knew* that was Kiki."

"Yeah," Ned said.

"I can't believe she walked right by me, and I didn't say anything." The soldier smacked himself in the head. "So stupid. I told myself there was no way that was her. It's too bad that livestream got interrupted. I would have liked to see what happened after." He turned and pointed to the middle of the store. "That's where she slipped, isn't it?"

Ned eyed John. "Maybe it *was* my fault."

A Chevy Impala pulled into the parking lot and circled near the front of the building. All eyes in the convenience store turned toward it.

Ned set his coffee down and stepped behind the counter. He grabbed his winter coat.

John eyed him. "Guess this is it."

"Guess so."

Ned reached for Travis and the cat swiped at him. "Hey, now. You didn't get spoiled with all that attention, did you?"

He picked up the cat and slipped him into a cat carrier. Ned had gone back to his bungalow and collected his things after receiving the phone call from the marshal service. There weren't many items—just the cat carrier and a couple of books were all he was taking.

Ned closed the gate and looked at the cat. "Let's forget the whole Cheddar Sprocket thing, okay?" He walked around the counter and headed toward the door.

"No sappy goodbye?" John asked.

Ned stopped at the door. For a moment, he considered saying something. Instead, he pushed the handle and stepped outside.

John laughed as Ned left the building.

***

U.S. Marshal Gayle Goodspeed shook her head, and her hands gripped the steering wheel tighter.

"It wasn't all my fault," Ned said.

"Right."

On the radio, a singer crooned about feeling the fire. It was the disco country music that the marshal liked. She was probably in heaven with the local radio station. When Ned reached for the volume button, Goodspeed slapped his hand.

"Don't," she said.

"It's a little loud."

"Why do you think that is?"

He looked out his side window.

"Another business ruined, Beau. That makes three." She held up as many fingers. "*Three.* You know how hard those are for us to develop?"

"I can imagine."

"No, you can't. If you could, you'd treat them better. And the hotline? You called the hotline and openly talked on it?"

"There was a situation.'"

Goodspeed's eyes narrowed. "Don't get smart."

"I'm just saying."

"I know what you're saying, and I'm saying to knock it off."

Ned sat silently for a couple of miles. When he thought the tension in the car had eased some, he said, "I didn't put myself on social media."

The marshal turned slightly. "Huh?"

"The video that was uploaded. I didn't do it."

She rolled her eyes. "I know that, but you just stood there while she took your dadburn picture. I saw it." Goodspeed frowned. "A bump on a log moves faster than you did."

"Where was I supposed to go?"

"Be creative," the marshal said. "Jump over the counter. Or hide in the freezer, for all I care."

"What about Grizzle?"

She checked the rearview mirror. "I'll give you that one. You didn't have nothing to do with him."

"Thank you."

"He came looking for your predecessor. Nothing you could have done about that, but you made his visit worse."

He stared at her. "How'd I do that? You saying I caused the blizzard, too?"

"Trying to be the hero is what you did." Goodspeed glanced at him. "What happened to you, Little Sister?"

"What do you mean?"

She shook her head. "This type of behavior isn't in your file. You keep sticking your nose where it doesn't belong. We figured you to be the anti-social type who'd keep to himself."

"I am. I do."

"For a guy who doesn't like people, you keep coming to their rescue."

"Maybe I'm trying to be better."

Goodspeed frowned. "Well, knock it off."

"Seriously?"

She waved a hand. "Or do it quieter. Why do you have to make so much noise when you do something good? You don't see me doing that—do you? No. You know why? Because I do my job and go about my day. Nobody ever needs to call in the National Guard for *me*."

The song on the radio ended, and the announcer came on. "*Whoo-whee, that song was a beaut. This is Winny and 92.9 FM helping you warm your tootsies on this cold winter morn.*" Her voice took on a level of officiousness. "*With the help of the Wyoming National Guard, members of local law enforcement apprehended those rascals involved with the daring robbery of the Casper National Bank of Wyoming. Boy, we are lucky to have them handsome fellas in blue.*"

Goodspeed smiled. "Seems they didn't get the memo about your participation."

Ned didn't care. He had other concerns.

A sign for Cheyenne loomed ahead. "Where are we headed?"

"South."

"No more winters?"

The marshal clicked her tongue against the back of her teeth. "Nope."

"Do you already have the next assignment ready?"

She didn't bother looking at him. "You think new identities grow on trees, Beau?" She hit her palm on the steering wheel. "It takes time and effort to put together something, especially the background. It's work."

"But you have an idea where we're going."

"Oh, I definitely have an idea."

"Am I going to like it?"

U.S. Marshal Gayle Goodspeed scowled. "Get real."

Beau Smith
returns in...

Cozy Up
to Terror

ABOUT THE AUTHOR

Besides writing the Cozy Up Series, Colin Conway is the author of the 509 Crime Stories, a series of novels set in Eastern Washington with revolving lead characters. They are standalone tales and can be read in any order.

Colin is also the co-author of the Charlie-316 series. The first book in the series, *Charlie-316*, is a political/crime thriller and has been described as "riveting and compulsively readable," "the real deal," and "the ultimate ride-along."

He served in the U.S. Army and later was an officer of the Spokane Police Department. He has owned a laundromat, invested in a bar, and run a karate school. Besides writing crime fiction, he is a commercial real estate broker.

Colin lives with his beautiful girlfriend, three wonderful children, and a codependent Vizsla that rules their world.

Learn more at colinconway.com.